"Unputdownable!! Blood, gore and suspense throughout. This is a book that was on my mind long after I finished it."

— *Pamela Z. Crutcher on Amazon*

"Incredibly engaging psychological thriller that you won't be able to put down."

— *Taylor on Amazon*

"Only a miracle will save them from the horror passing through."

— *Sharon Lopes*

"Very graphic and disturbing in the best way! If you like to delve into the minds of twisted, sadistic killers you will love this book."

— *AMR on Amazon*

"A great read, the true fact is there are sickos out there just like this man."

— *Kindle Customer*

"One of the most terrifying books I've ever read, scared me so much, I stayed up until I finished."

— *Cinder on Amazon*

"I cringed and kept going to the next page."

— *Gaillee on Amazon*

"The terror, the suspense, the gore... It was like watching a train wreck... you couldn't look away no matter how much you wanted to."
— *Amazon Customer*

"The pacing was fast, with an almost ominous terror building with each page."
— *Mark A Cinense on Amazon*

"Be prepared to lose sleep turning page after page long into the night."
— *Karen on Amazon*

"Humanity can sometimes bare some of the most grotesque of creatures. A pure psychological thriller."
— *John McNabb on Amazon*

"A true horror novel. It is not for the faint at heart. I have no complaints of this brilliantly written book."
— *Jerminator on Amazon*

"Sadistic, gruesome serial killer so beware... it's very graphic, but that's what helps make the book so real."
— *Amazon Customer*

"Did I like it? No! It terrified me! Was it skillful writing? Without a doubt."
— *S.H. David on Amazon*

Passing Through

By
R.W.K. Clark

Published in the United States by Clarkltd.
Po Box 45313 Rio Rancho, NM 87174
info@clarkltd.com

Edition 1
United States Copyright Office
TX 8-503-424 November 2017

Library of Congress Control Number: 2017919791

International Standard Book Numbers
ISBN-13: 978-1948312097 (Hardcover)
ISBN-13: 978-1948312103(Paperback)
ISBN-13: 978-1948312011 (Amazon)
ASIN: B078S5BP8S (Kindle)

/180425

ACKNOWLEDGMENTS

I dedicate this novel to my wonderful readers and for all the amazing people I've met and those I haven't. To my family and loved ones, all your support will not be forgotten.

Thank you

PROLOGUE

The young teen sat, bound in the chair in front of the searing hot fireplace. He was tied tightly with a nylon rope that seemed to be cutting him in two, in more places than one. He had never been in such physical pain in his life.

In front of him were three dead bodies. One of them was his beloved girlfriend of two years. The other two were her friends from school. The four of them had come here for spring break fun and games; it was her parents' cabin, a big, beautiful place, and it would be the perfect vacation for all four of them.

But something had gone terribly wrong. Yesterday, a stranger had come, and he had put them through twenty-four hours of rape, torture, and torment like none of them ever knew existed. Now, the girls lay dead, ripped open from their groins to their necks. One of them had her head cut nearly clean off, and they had been raped in every way possible.

The young teen had been forced to watch, duct tape tight over his mouth, and his eyes pinned open with large safety pins. All he could do was cry as he listened to the stranger in the other room. The stranger was cooking something in the microwave and eating, and in between bites, he would sing along to a song on the radio. The young teen wasn't fooling himself; when the stranger was done eating, he was sure he would be next. The young teen was prepared to join his girlfriend in whatever afterlife she had entered. He wanted to die, because if he lived, he would never forget a single second of what he had witnessed, and he simply could not live with that.

Tears continued to fall down his face, and he hated himself for his own powerlessness and weakness. He wanted to die.

Suddenly, the radio in the kitchen went off, and the stranger rounded the corner. He stopped and stared at the three dead girls, a smile glued to his face. The young teen stared at the stranger, disgusted, as he realized that the guy was getting aroused just looking at their corpses. The teen wanted to vomit, but he would choke to death if he did. He glanced the other direction in an effort to ignore the sick dirtball that was standing there.

"Aren't they beautiful?" the stranger asked him, amused. "Oh, you would have enjoyed it all, had you been me. You know, I was planning to off you too, young man, but now I'm full and I'm bored. I think it's time to hit the road, so he said his goodbyes, and left. The young teen was doing the best he could to scream through the tape. He was going to die there, and he knew it.

But he was wrong. A few days later, the girlfriend's parents had the police do a check, and they were found. The young teen alive, the three girls dead, and everyone's life forever changed.

R.W.K. Clark

CHAPTER 1

"Keller!"

The inmate slowly opened his eyes, but not another muscle in his body moved. He always maintained his serenity, even when those in authority over his body were demanding control of him, as they were doing now. There was no reason to jump up and disrupt himself in excitement; there was a very specific process to all things in the penitentiary, even something as small as being called out of your cell by a corrections officer for some random, unknown reason. He wouldn't give them any more control than they already had. As usual, he waited for the loud, hollow echo of the lock on his cell to sound, signifying they had opened it.

He had been dreaming, a terrible dream about something that had happened to him when he was a boy, something his father had done to his mother, maybe? He never could be sure anymore; Keller lost touch with the reality of his life long ago. Some things he knew to be real, while others almost seemed like something he was told, or something he made up in the fantasy; he lived deep inside his mind. Anyway, it didn't matter that the dream had been a bad one; he despised when the corrections officers and buzzers and bells interrupted his dreams and plans.

Suddenly a metallic bang sound filled the air. The electronically-controlled iron bolt slid from its place and slammed into the open position. Keller sat up, stretched out slowly, and swung his feet to the floor. He slid his stockinged feet into his prison-issue canvas slip-on sneakers that were already showing signs of significant wear, even though he had received them new a couple of months ago.

He stood and stretched again, a slight smile coming over his lips. He loved to take his time, to make them wait as long as possible, even if it was only a few extra seconds. They had too much power, anyway; it was far better to waste as much of their lives as they were wasting of his. The fact was, Keller was the one with the power; what they had was nothing more than illusions of grandeur, and he found it hilarious to play with them the way he did.

"Keller! Move it!" the intercom voice echoed throughout the corridor.

He stepped to the door of his cell, as it slid open until it slammed against the end of its track. He then stepped out into the cold tile and cinder block corridor. There he stopped, hands behind his back, and stared straight ahead; it was policy to do that silly stuff, after all.

The door reversed, slamming loudly on its track.

Several other inmates, whose cells were running along the same side of the hall, began to whine and grumble at his lack of concern for their peace, but he shut out their voices; heck with them.

He resumed his straight-backed position, clasping his hands behind him once again. It was just after suppertime, around six-thirty in the evening. He stared out the windows which lined the bare cinder block wall across from the row of cells. The sky was really beginning to darken early now; it would be dark in no time. November, December, and January had always been his favorite months because of the early, long-lasting darkness at night. It gave men like him plenty of time to play under the cover of the night. Night time was the best time to play if you had a nature that was easily bored.

"Turn left and approach the block door!" The intercom-streamed voice echoed once again, this time a bit more calmly.

Like a loyal soldier, Keller did as he was told, and proceeded to walk down the long corridor, past the other cells and the smart aleck comments being shot in his direction from other offenders. He wasn't there to make friends. Bunch of juvenile sissies.

At the far-end of the corridor was a massive, heavy door, constructed entirely of thick steel, and like everything else in the prison, it was painted standard gray. It had a small window about a foot-and-a-half from the top that measured about eight inches by eight inches, and it held a pane of glass that was reinforced with wire on the inside. This door, like all the others at the Virginia Maximum Correctional Institute, was controlled electronically by a corrections officer that sat in a glass bubble on the other side. As he waited for them to buzz him through, Keller muttered something about how rough it must be to sit on your fat butt and eat doughnuts all day long, giving orders.

The door buzzed obnoxiously, prompting him to grab it by the handle and give the heavy door a violent tug. The latch popped audibly, stopping the profane buzzing. Keller pulled it all the way open and stepped through, letting it slam shut, automatically locking, behind him.

One of the best-known corrections officers was standing there in all his glory, his brown and tan uniform hugging his pot belly tightly. He stood about six-foot-four, was completely bald, and had a nicely groomed handlebar mustache that seemed to trickle down from his upper lip to his chin on both sides. The man smirked in Keller's direction.

"Follow me. We have a change in your work assignment, and there is quite a bit to go over before you can begin tonight."

Keller said nothing; he simply followed the huge guy like he was told. His mind raced with slurs and bloody thoughts that consisted of what he would ever do to this particular corrections officer if he was ever alone with him and the circumstances were right. These people had no idea what he was capable of; they had seen pictures and heard testimonies given by whimpering lowlifes who were blackened by their own personal sins, but had never been caught. None of it was real to the prison staff. Their jobs didn't begin until after the blood, guts, and hearings. They simply came to work every day, dealt with the dirtballs with their guns and sticks and chains, and then they went home to their wives and kids. What a waste...

They walked down several cold hallways, past several doors, and finally stopped outside the Inmate Work Detail office, which was in the admin section of the main building. This time of day the only people here for work were the corrections officers; all the administration staff and counselors had gone home at five. Whatever was going on, it was a last-minute thing.

The corrections officer unlocked the office, opened the door, and held it, signifying with a nod that Keller should enter. He did, then stood there, still and silent, waiting to be told what to do next. The corrections officer walked around the desk in the middle of the small office, sat down, then nodded toward a chair gruffly; Keller sat.

"Our night laundry guy let his criminal thinking get away from him, so he lost his job," the corrections officer began, sitting back in the chair and crossing his arm over his chest. "Now, we all know who you are and what you are capable of, but your boss, the Sergeant, seems to think that you can be trusted to take the position. But the lieutenant wants me to have a good long talk with you and feel you out before we move you up. This laundry shift requires a lot of trust, Keller. Now, I admit, you have kept your nose good and clean for the last five years, but you're a monster, and we both know that. So, why should we let you be alone for eight hours a night down in laundry? Why should we trust you with Reception & Delivery?"

Keller didn't smile, but he sure wanted to. He couldn't believe his ears. Were they really going to offer the night shift to him? The corrections officer had just asked a good question: why would they let him have the position. Were they all out of their minds? He had been coveting that shift for years, but it wasn't because he was trying to move up the inmate corporate ladder. He thought about his answer, his eyes skimming from the corrections officer to the items on the desk, and back again. He was able to easily take in the details of every item on the desk, since there was nothing but a plastic in and out file with one sheet of paper lying lonely, waiting for attention. No pen holders, no desk lamp, not even a blotter. Oh, yeah. That's right, he was in prison. He chuckled silently to himself and mentally shook his head.

"You know, Mr. I've thought about how nice that night shift would be lots of times." Inmate Keller clicked his tongue against his cheek. "I don't think there's a man here that hasn't. So, this is my offered reward for being a 'good boy'? Well, I have to say, I'm much obliged, sir. The fact is, if I'm spending the rest of my life here, I might as well make it as pleasant for myself as possible, even if that includes little promotions here and there. I mean, if the tables were turned, wouldn't you do the same?"

The correctional officer didn't smile, or even nod. He simply studied the convict across from him, wondering if his calm, controlled demeanor could be trusted in any way. He had been a corrections officer with the state prison system for nearly twenty years, and he hadn't met a convict yet who uttered a single word you could trust. Even the octogenarian lifers that they housed were slippery as eels when your back was turned. Judging from the horrific truths that were Elliot James Keller's crimes, he was absolutely no different from any of them.

"Well, the tables aren't turned, and you deserve to be dead, but instead, well, here we are."

∞

Virginia Max was a maximum-security prison, and one of the most secure in the nation. There had been an old, mansion-like building where this one stood now, but it had been razed and replaced with consistent upgrades in rebuilding and technology as the years passed. This was one prison that was able to hold its water, and it was able because of the vermin that lived behind its razor wire and armed corrections officer towers.

Virginia supported the death penalty, but Keller had gotten away without that particular consequence happening by the skin of his teeth. The man was smart, manipulative, and had a way of buttering up those in charge that could benefit him that none of them really understood. The corrections officer didn't want to understand the guy. To him, that meant diving down to his level of insanity and monstrosity, and he wanted nothing to do with it. Heck with being a counselor or group leader; he'd stick to corrections officering these rabid dirtballs, and he'd always hope for a chance to bust a cap in one of them before he retired.

His eyes continued to scan Keller, up and down, considering the man before him, what he was capable of, and the position he would be taking in the prison laundry.

∞

Keller was a triple murderer of three young ladies. They happened to be vacationing alone at a cabin belonging to the family of one of the girls during spring break six-years back. It was supposed to be a fun, footloose time for the four young adults, but it turned into a nightmare when Keller happened to come upon the cabin after breaking down at one of the nearby Appalachian Trailheads. He had hiked himself right out of the national scenic trail's property; suddenly, the cabin was there. Keller pounced like a hungry wildcat. Armed and bored, by his own admission, the man had taken a small group of kids hostage right in the cabin, forcing them into submission with fear for their lives. Keller bound the young man, tying him to a chair, and forced him to watch as he shot each of the young ladies in the foot, disabling them. He proceeded to beat each of the girls with the butt of his gun, then raped each of their lifeless bodies repeatedly while the young man was forced to watch in horror. Keller had put safety pins through the boy's eyelids, then taped them up with duct tape, running it in two long strips that went over the top of his head and down his back. The young man miraculously survived the ordeal, claiming that Keller told him he would let him live because he had grown bored of their games, and after such a good time, he was tired. He left him there, tied to the chair in front of the bodies. They were all discovered by the owners when the telephone repeatedly went unanswered for a full-day.

∞

The thought of Keller's past made the corrections officer want to puke all over the guy. Now, the sergeant feels that this guy should have control of the laundry, alone down there every night. Sure, there was no way of escaping, with the corrections officer constantly coming in to observe deliveries and the basic operations. But to work in the laundry was also a privilege; you came in contact with outsiders, such as delivery men, food truck drivers, the US Mail, and countless others. The prison was a tiny working town, so to speak. The prison was also surrounded by high fences and razor wire, all electrified, and at every junction in the fence around the property stood a manned corrections officer tower, alert and armed.

Lights were everywhere, and at the first hint of a breach, alarms begin to deafen.

The corrections officer's problem with Keller getting the job was simple: the man was a monster. He should have received the death penalty for his crimes, but thanks to a smooth-talking psych doctor who had managed to load him up on medication and give persuasive expert opinions on the stand, Keller had dodged that much-deserved bullet. The entire point he was put here by the great state of Virginia was because he was a sick dirtball that should not be around other human beings, but he was also too sick to put down. He is a rabid dog, a poisonous snake, neither of which can ever be trusted.

But the Warden Jaffrey called the ultimate shots, and this 'promotion' was her call all the way, not to mention she had even been enthusiastic about it. Wanda Jaffrey was fairly new to her position herself, having just taken over as warden two short years ago. She also happened to be the first woman warden Virginia Max had ever known, and she had some pretty new and flighty ideas when it came to convicts and rehabilitation. She wanted to give a bit of trust, to get a bit of trust, even inside the walls of a prison that housed nothing but the most violent of animals in the state, not to mention the world. But even though the men here would likely never see the light of day, she believed they could live and function happily, free of their violence and burdens, through rehabilitation. Maybe so, but would any of us ever really know? What is real with these people, and what is a mask? They were sickened criminals.

But in the end, the corrections officer was just an officer, and he was there to carry the crap downhill instead of allowing it to roll. It also didn't help that the previous night laundry guy, who had been handling laundry for the last eight years, tried to commit suicide after his wife of twenty five years decided she couldn't live loyally to a convict, quarter-century in or not. She 'Dear John-ed' him, leaving the warden no choice.

After several long, quiet minutes of thought, the corrections officer offered more of a smirk than a half-smile and clasped his hands in front of him on the desk. He had never really been one to pull punches, and he had no favorites or pets when it came to these losers. Not even the small-timers could get in his good graces. Oh, he could be pleasant enough, but his pleasantries went no deeper than the sound of his voice. He hated them, he hated them all, and if he could, not a one of them would exist on the planet.

"Warden Jaffrey seems to think you're the shoe-in, Keller; you've got her snowed, but good, though I don't get how you managed to do it. I personally don't believe that you have enough time under your belt for such trust, but I don't run the show. As a matter of fact, you'll die here, and I don't think that even then you'll be any better for the time you've spent or the taxpayers' money you've wasted. You're excrement to me, and nothing more."

The corrections officer paused and held the murderer's eyes for effect; the man held his steadily and calmly in return, no expression on his face. "The fact of the matter is, and I can admit it, you never have been a behavior problem of any kind, not from the beginning, and to me, that's what makes you so dangerous. No problems when they arrested you, and never in court or during your trial. Not in jail, and not a whimper since you transferred here. For someone who did what you did, well, I just can't figure you out, except to guess that you have something up your prison-issue sleeve. So, because of your self-control and steady cooperation with programming, and because I don't have a thing to say about it, the job is yours. We need you to start tonight at eleven. Be sure to set your alarm, because none of us are gonna do you any favors by waking you up. All of us are hoping you oversleep and get fired before you ever set foot down there tonight."

Keller offered a smile, though it was tight around the edges. He sat forward, his elbows resting on his thighs.

"Well, sir, you tell the warden I said thank you. I know she's a busy woman, so I won't bother her." An expectant look crossed his face, but he remained silent until the corrections officer stood.

But the corrections officer didn't stand, he simply held Keller's gaze. This was a mistake, he just knew it. He didn't know why the guy bothered him so much. No, it was the man himself. To put it simply, the corrections officer didn't trust him as far as he could throw him.

"Tell me something, inmate Keller," the corrections officer finally said in a strong, yet soft, voice. "Why did you do it?"

Now a sincere smile came over the murderer's face, and the corrections officer actually saw his eyes soften a bit. "Now, you know as well as anyone else on the face of the earth... why do any of us cause ourselves any kind of trouble, big or small? Why do we drunk drive, or hit our wives, or shoplift, or even torture little, insignificant animals for entertainment? I'll tell you exactly why, Boss.

"Because sometimes messing up is simply a lot more funny and entertaining than anything else you have to do at the time. Sometimes, you do it because you can."

CHAPTER 2

The cell door gave its signature slam behind Keller as he crossed the tiny area he called home. Reaching his bunk, he sat down and stared across the cell and out the bars, focusing his eyes on a single cinder block that had basically served as his best friend since he had been at Virginia Max; he had the block literally memorized. Every crack, chipped paint spot, and individual difference were etched into his mind like a fond childhood memory, not that he had any of those. The fact was, Elliot Keller used the block, and its memory, to not only focus but to calm himself when he felt the urge to blow, which was more often than anyone in the prison knew of. Every day, he would stare at the block at random times, shutting out all else and making it his entire world for however long it took to calm his pounding heart and screaming rage. As a result, no matter where he happened to be in the facility, if he felt the rage coming, or if he was tempted to play with the blood and guts of another inmate or corrections officer, he thought of the block, and the recall soothed his temptations. To put it simply, the block had kept him from continuing his rampages, had kept him out of the hole, and had ultimately gotten him the night laundry position he had wanted for so long.

He couldn't believe the time had finally come, but it had. Keller had been waiting patiently, biding his time and subtly kissing up to prison staff by simply minding his p's and q's, all in hopes of landing the much-desired night laundry position. Now it was his; all of his focusing and refusing himself the joy and fun he wanted had given him the result he yearned for. Tonight, at ten-forty-five, a corrections officer would escort him to the laundry. Soon, that position would spell out freedom for him; all it would take was a bit of fine tuning when it came to timing and small details. He had nothing but time and patience; after all, he had been in the prison nearly five years after having sat in jail attending his own trial hearings for a year prior to that. Yes, if doing time did anything for a man, it taught him patience, but only if he let it.

There was a massive variety of other life experiences which had done the same for him over the course of his life. Like the times his real father had locked him into the dank storage area in the basement with the dirt floor when he was two or three. He would keep Keller down there for doing things like dribbling on the toilet seat, or walking around with one of his shoes untied. The man had been a brute, and none of his punishments had anything to do with actual discipline, or the need to have a well-behaved son. No, the elder Keller got off on the screaming, crying, and begging that his punishments incited. Sometimes, his father would even sit in a metal folding chair outside of the room in the basement, laughing and eating platefuls of aromatic food that had been prepared by his bloodied and beaten mother. His father would ask him, over and over as he laughed, if he thought the fried chicken smelled good, and wouldn't he just love some?

Keller vowed he'd kill that dirtball someday, and he would do his mother at the same time, just for letting it take place.

He broke his dead stare and slipped off his shoes, then lay down on his bed. He could hear the sound of a couple of other inmates who lived on M Corridor, which was his own corridor. Someone was shuffling a deck of cards, and he could hear a low conversation consisting of what he imagined were war stories of crime. Every now and then, a snicker or full laugh could be heard from them, giving away their conversations. Convicts loved to boast of their conquests to each other, but he knew better. His adventures in life were his own, and he loved each and every terrible act as if they were his children. He would share them with no one.

The cards were being shuffled again. Often, the inmates in two neighboring cells would get together at the point where their cells met and converse or play dice or cards through the bars, using the corridor floor as their table. The inmates on M Corridor were not supposed to be doing this; they were considered the worst of the worst and were to be segregated except when on job detail, or when they were taking 'rehabilitative' classes and counseling. Suddenly, Keller laughed out loud, and the idiots with the cards went silent for a second at the sound. Keller shook his head at their curiosity and waited for the shuffling to begin once again.

Everyone at Virginia Max was crazy, in their own way and on their own level. No one did the things these men had done without being 'off,' even if they were well aware of the differences between right and wrong. Even Elliot Keller knew that anyone who would rape and murder was sick, even if they did it simply to get off on it. Yeah, he was nuts, and he was dangerous, and he loved every single minute of it. The look in the eyes of his victims was like a fine hollandaise poured over the very best asparagus. Their screams were like a perfectly grilled medium rare

Porterhouse. Their deaths were like winning the lottery, and all of it got his rocks off with such potency that he thought the top of his head might blow off at any time. He loved to reminisce about the good old days…

Yes, he was feared, and he was keenly aware of it, though he had done nothing to instigate the emotion in other inmates. His reputation preceded him, and it was as simple as that. He kept to himself almost completely, never intentionally intimidating or threatening. The only real communication he did with others, he did solely out of need. For instance, some things required communication when working or in group or one-on-one sessions with one's counselor. For him, these interactions were all business, and he kept all of his words centered on the topic at the time. Keller never offered information about himself to other prisoners; he wasn't here to make friends. The only time he spoke about his crime, or any other he had committed, was in a one-on-one with the counselor or in group, and then his words were brief and extremely calculated and superficial. It was important to appear to be seeking remorse and repentance if he wanted to gain trust, so he gave them just enough to make them happy. In reality, while he divulged any detail, he was simultaneously imagining what he would like to do to one of them or the other.

He was never connected emotionally to anything that came out of his mouth in this place.

He had never been connected to anything anywhere, and Keller liked it that way. They didn't need to know any more about him than they already did, because they carried around little textbooks that told them what he was about, and not one of them was all the way correct in his theories. But they were close enough that his thoughts could be revealed and his plans spoiled simply by speaking too much about any one thing. He treaded lightly and thoughtfully, and it was all for him and him alone.

His mind drifted to the laundry job again. When he first arrived at Virginia Max, his assigned work detail had been lousy. He had been working in the prison kitchen, where all newcomers worked. They all started in the dish room, then moved up to floors and deep cleaning. If you didn't ruffle feathers, moving up was easy, and it hadn't taking him long before he was put in charge of the dry storage room, a cushy job.

There were those in the world, most men and women, in fact, who were just like him, but none of them had the nerve to bring their dreams and fantasies to life the way he did. Not Keller; he was real. He was true to himself and his own mind. Oh well! if they didn't get it while they sat up on their high horses and pointed down at him, judging and shaking their heads.

He would love to show them all what reality was all about.

Now his thoughts shifted back to the institution that he had called home for the last several years. Keller really couldn't complain about Virginia Max, regardless of all the technicalities and phonies; of all the prisons in the state, this one was really the most comfortable, especially when one considered the criminals there and the level of security under which they did live. The majority of inmates were violent, and most of them were doing twenty-five to life, or even multiple life sentences, and that was if they had escaped the death penalty, as he had. The place consisted of corridor units, each housing the most violent, or the criminally insane. Basically, those who couldn't be trusted lived on the corridors because they were classified as unable to cohabitate with others peacefully. Other prisoners were housed in different 'block units,' depending on their crimes. They were mid-level criminals who were usually serving fifteen to twenty-five. They were men who had a light at the end of their tunnel: they might just see freedom before they die.

Virginia Max also had inmates who were housed on the psychiatric unit. Their crimes were attributed to their mental state, so while they did their time, they were pumped full of drugs and put in restraints. They got to go out into an enclosed yard with grass and benches on occasion, but they were heavily watched so they wouldn't hurt each other. Some of these men would get out; most would die in the stinking, filthy unit they lived in.

A hand full of men were the ones in the 'hole.' They went in and out, in and out, doing their hole time for some infraction or other, getting back into population, then doing something else. They were defiant and didn't have the brains to know when to shut their mouths; they were the attention seekers who would act up just to make their friends laugh. Keller didn't have that problem; he had been doing time in one way or another since the day he was born.

But now, after five years, he had a light at the end of his own tunnel. He wasn't sure of the specific details, and had yet to form a solid plan in his mind, but his new laundry position was his ticket out of Virginia Max. It might take a week, or maybe a month; it could take a year or more. It didn't matter how long it took, Keller was going to walk out of this place, and he was going to have a little fun when he did. They would catch him, but he didn't care. It was his duty to escape; what kind of good criminal didn't think about, and attempt, to escape from a life sentence?

Elliot Keller closed his eyes and steadied his mind. He wasn't going to just attempt to escape, he would get the job done. Then, after they caught him, and he faced the new charges, he would return with a smile on his face, a brand-new memory of warm blood and terrified screams etched onto his heart forever.

R.W.K. Clark

CHAPTER 3

Another snow storm was about to hit the town of Thompson Trails and it was promising to be a doozy. The town was on emergency alert, and though the snow was barely just beginning to fall, the entire population had already bought provisions and locked themselves up safely in their homes, preparing for the worst.

In the meantime, there were many residents leaving, and some were arriving to see family. After all, with the storm brewing, it was best to get to holiday destinations ahead of time. A single bus was due to arrive and do one final drop-off and pick up, then the rest of the schedule would be cancelled until the storm was over and the roads had been cleared.

Sheriff Robert Brown loved his town. When inclement weather hit, he always made it a habit to go around and check on every last resident. He was doing that now, at the same time the bus was just pulling in for its final Thompson Trails stop.

Sheriff Brown pulled down a gravel lane toward the Martin cabin. The snow was beginning to cover the drive with a fine dusting, so now was the perfect time to stop and do a check. He climbed out of his truck and knocked on their door. The Martins lived in the big, beautiful cabin year-around, and they refused to leave, even in adverse conditions. He just wanted to make sure they had everything they needed.

"Howdy, Bob," Jake Martin greeted as he opened the door and let the Sheriff in.

"Jake, mornin'," Sheriff Brown nodded at Janet Martin, who was crocheting next to the fire, and their pretty fifteen-year-old daughter appeared to be playing with her smartphone. "Just stopping to check in. You know, it's gonna be a bad one, don't you agree?"

"Worst one yet," Jake replied. "We're just gonna stay in and bond, if you know what I mean."

Brown nodded. "Best bet for us all, I think. Smells good in here; what did y'all have for breakfast?"

Their daughter spoke up and crinkled her nose. "Biscuits... ugh."

The adults laughed.

"Can I get you a coffee, Bob?" Janet asked.

"No thank you, ma'am," he replied. "Much obliged, but I still have a number of families to check on, and the missus is expecting me on time for dinner."

"Be sure to give Rose our love." Janet replied.

Jake made his way to the door to show the sheriff out. "Sure appreciate your concern. We're all gonna have to get together for some canasta when this all passes."

"Sounds good to me," Bob Brown said with a tip of his hat. "Well, I'm out of here. Lock her up and keep safe, y'all."

He left and got into his truck, turned around, and headed back up the drive. The snow was coming down good now, huge flakes falling like mad, and blowing wind taking complete control. Since he had been inside, which was about five minutes, the snow had accumulated at least an inch.

"Yep, it's a bad one, all right," he muttered as he pulled out of the drive and onto the highway.

∞

Donna Welk turned the key in the keyhole of the office door and rushed inside, slamming the door quickly behind her. She stopped and let out the long, ragged breath she'd been holding, then brushed the snow off the shoulders of her parka before taking it off and hanging it on the hook behind the main desk. Sitting down, she shivered once more for good measure; if the weather was like this in the first week of November, she was dreading what the rest of the Virginia winter would be like.

She quickly glanced at the clock: nine-fifteen in the morning. Donna highly doubted that they would have any stop-in guests today because of the weather. Usually during this time of year, the flow of guests was steady, but slow. Right now, Donna and her husband didn't have a single cabin rented out, and she couldn't see anyone stopping by with interest today. If the weatherman was right, they were likely to be empty for the remainder of the week. It would hurt the pocket book, but it was better than having people die trying to rent a cabin near the Appalachian Trail just to say they did. Guests would wait; life did not.

She and Rick had purchased the old cluster of cabins two years ago, both of them harboring big dreams of taking the trailhead at Thompson Trails by storm. The business, and the cabins, all needed a lot of work; the accommodations all were in desperate need of serious renovations, also the business itself was in a bit of debt that would take months, if not years, to eliminate. So far, the couple hadn't done too badly; last year they remodeled all the units and had the grounds freshly landscaped. They also added a small playground for kids, and then started renting canoes to guests for use in the lake out back. After advertising unbeatable specials for frequent visitors, they began to climb out of the hole that the previous owner had dug for them. In the beginning, getting back in the black was an overwhelming prospect; now it looked like things would be cleared up in the next eighteen months.

"But not if we have many days like this," Donna muttered as she pulled out the checkbook so she could pay the bills.

The small town of Thompson Trails had known the storm was on its way, but like everyone on Earth, they all hoped it would either dissipate or pass before it reached them. It hadn't, and last night, the first flakes began to fall. When Donna and Rick woke, the town was covered in a blanket of glistening white snow, and Rick had to quickly dress and get out the snow-blower so the lot would be clear for potential stop-in guests.

Donna got down to business in the office.

Suddenly, the door flew open and Rick rushed in. The wind fought him hard when he tried to close it, and he had to use all of his weight to get it closed. When he did, he turned around and leaned against it, his face red and his breathing labored.

"I had to run over here or I was going to get blown away!" He unzipped his coat and started to remove it. "Why don't you have the radio on, Donna? They said the main road through town is going to be closing in a few hours; the snow is going to last for days! It's going to close all the way to the interstate both ways until the snow begins to die and they can clear the roads!"

Donna groaned and sat back hard in her desk chair. "Rick! We're right in the middle! Well, so much for any guests for a day or two. I guess now is the time for me to catch up on getting those hard files on the computer, eh?"

"Good idea. You know, the funny thing is that you're probably gonna get all that scanned in, and then ten years from now, we'll realize that we never even looked back into those records once." Rick hung up his coat and rubbed his hands together. "At least the lot is clear for now, you know, just in case we get lucky or something."

Donna chuckled and shook her head. "Ever the optimist, my husband."

"Someone has to be. Say, maybe if it stays like this, we can participate together in a little, you know, hanky-panky."

Donna turned and grabbed one of three boxes of files stacked out of sight behind her desk. There had been more than twenty boxes when they bought the place; she had three left. The previous owners hadn't used computers or technology for recordkeeping at all, and now Donna was cleaning up the mess.

With a shake of her head, she replied, "This is all the hanky-panky I'm getting into today."

"Well, Dear, I'm going to warm up then hit that lot again. It's going to be a never-ending task for a while, I'm afraid." He paused and glanced at the guest courtesy table, which sat behind him in the lobby. The table offered packaged donuts, cookies, fruit, as well as coffee. "You didn't make any java? Woman! Do you want any?"

"If you're making it."

Rick stuck his tongue out and headed to the pot. Donna watched her husband fondly as he filled the pot, then scooped coffee into the basket. Regardless of the work and the cost, she believed that they made a wonderful decision when they bought the Virginia Trailhead Cabins. If nothing else, the purchase and move had taken both of their minds off the recent loss of pregnancy and the subsequent knowledge that there would be no more chances of parenting for them. Donna and Rick had come quite harshly to the knowledge that they would never have children due to the weakness of her uterine lining, and in their grief, they decided to forget about children and buy the cabins. She didn't believe it was a mistake; after two years, the grief had faded for them substantially, and the couple had made the small lake getaway near the Appalachian Trail, their child. Donna and Rick had found happiness after terrible loss, and it was because of this place. Sometimes, when Rick brought up lovemaking, as he just did, her stomach actually turned. It wasn't that she didn't like fooling around, but for some reason, she couldn't separate it from childbearing, and they both knew that wasn't going to happen for them.

The small cabin resort had changed their lives for the better. Rick and Donna relocated, started life anew, and began to make new friends. It hadn't taken them long to fit right in, and now they were considered 'locals' by the others, much to their surprise. The fact that the handful of native Thompson Trails residents didn't take kindly to new settlers was well-known and broadcasted, but for some reason, the couple belonged there, like a couple of toes in a nicely broken-in shoe.

Both of them went about their tasks, with Rick making coffee and Donna focusing on the backed-up paperwork and the computer. In a few minutes, the sound of tires crunching over the rapidly accumulating snow grabbed her attention and she turned to the window. Sheriff Robert Brown was pulling into the lot in his big pickup plow, and Donna was not surprised; the short, stocky man liked to touch base with all of his 'people' when the weather was acting up, just in case they had come into a spot of trouble and were unable to ask for help.

"Rick?" She turned her head to see her husband just coming out of the men's room, fastening his belt. "Bob's outside. Better ask him in for some coffee."

Grabbing his coat, he replied, "Sure thing." Rick opened the office door and stepped outside, waving his arm at the sheriff, and Donna heard him shout. "Hey, Bob! Beautiful day we're having!"

With a smile and a shake of her head, Donna turned her attention back to her work. Even in the midst of a storm, she felt peaceful. Of all the choices she faced with Rick in their marriage, moving to Thompson Trails had been the best one they made. She hadn't regretted it for a moment, and she didn't think she ever would.

∞

"So, I was told a resort company out of Richmond was planning to level the old grocery building to put a strip mall in, which would ultimately bring more business to the small town and give it a bit of a bigger dot on the maps." Avery continued.

"You know what, Rose? Believe it or not, I think Darren actually got the last thing I put on the list for him to pick up from Donneley's Pass." Avery Rush had a smile on her face, and this made Rose Brown happy.

"Usually, he'll forget most anything, but he's been so good lately about taking care of me. Sometimes I feel guilty about it."

Rose patted her on the shoulder. "Just try to understand he loves you."

Avery did understand the stress; as a matter of fact, it made her physically ill to have to tell her husband she was pregnant. Her husband was carrying around a lot of responsibilities already; being the deputy was a hard job, and now, they were pregnant and needed a bigger house to boot.

She could do nothing to stop the onslaught of responsibilities that Darren Rush was taking on, and now with a child on the way. As a matter of fact, she had been consistently ill since the pregnancy, but in the last couple of weeks, Avery had begun to feel better, and the only reason she found remained inside of her.

Now, here she sat with Rose, drinking coffee and finally going through the cards for the baby shower that Darren had brought to her from Donneley's Pass. As she had said, it appeared he had gotten every last item on the list.

"Avery, don't you forget about that appointment you have at noon with Dr. Frazer," Rose said in a motherly fashion. "I know you are feeling better, and it's obvious by your behavior, but in this situation, I think it's imperative that you follow through dear. Who knows? Maybe he'll tell you if it's a boy or a girl?"

Avery glanced at her watch. "Yes, I should go home and jump into the shower, I suppose. Listen, Rosie, don't you worry a thing about all these cards. As soon as I get back, I will give you a call, I need to do a bit more unpacking as well. So, tomorrow, we can get back to work and soon the cards will be out of your hair." She turned to the lady and took her into an embrace; Rose hugged her back hard.

"You're a great help," she said. "You know as well as I do that I wouldn't have made it through all of this myself without you and Bob."

"I know dear, now scoot."

Avery gave the woman a peck on the cheek and disappeared home.

An hour later, Avery was leaving the house with her husband, who had returned for the sole purpose of driving her to her appointment in Donneley's Pass.

∞

Darren Rush sat in the waiting room at Dr. Frazer's office, waiting patiently for his wife with a magazine in his lap. He wasn't reading it, just blindly flipping the pages every few minutes. His mind was on Avery. After all of the morning sickness, she had been a mess, and her state of mind, including physical sickness, had lasted nearly two whole months. As of late, though, she seemed a bit better: more cheerful, and almost like she might get back to her real self soon.

The door leading to the back opened up, and Avery stepped out. She looked a bit pale, but when she saw Darren, a smile covered her face. He smiled back and stood up.

"Are we ready?" he asked.

"Just about," she replied softly. "Dr. Frazer wants me to make a follow-up appointment. If you want to go start the truck, I'll be out in just a bit."

Darren nodded and left, Avery watching him as he went. At last, she turned to the pretty young receptionist. "The doctor wants me to schedule another appointment."

The girl looked up at her with a look that resembled both happiness and cheer. "I know, dear. He filled me in. I am glad you're feeling better. When's a good time for you?"

The two women narrowed down a time, working around all of the chores that Darren and Avery were involved with due to their pending move. Avery kept a smile on her face the entire time, but inside she felt like she was falling apart. When they were finished, she tucked the little appointment card in her purse, plastered another smile on, and went out to the truck and her waiting husband.

As they drove back to Thompson Trails, Darren asked about her appointment. "So, what did Dr. Frazer say?"

"Well," Avery replied lightly, "he thinks I'm doing better, both mentally and physically."

"Great!" Darren patted her thigh. "So, what's the follow up for?"

Avery shrugged and picked at some invisible lint on her coat. "Just to make sure my body is handling the change all right, I guess."

"What a relief!" Darren patted her leg again. "I sure love you, Avery. I have to tell you, you are the strongest woman I know, and I couldn't be more blessed to have you for a wife."

"I feel the same way about you, Darren."

They tooled the rest of the way back to their new home with the radio on, humming and holding hands with each passing mile. Darren seemed happy enough; Avery glanced at him continually out of the corner of her eye, smiling.

∞

The Rushes got home from Donneley's Pass late that afternoon. Avery had spent the remainder of the day unpacking and sorting. Darren was transporting boxes and other small items to their new home while she worked. With each return trip, he would pile more stuff into the truck. Rose had given them several items of furniture that she had kept stored in a large garage out back, and all of these things pretty much gave the Rushes a brand-new start. It should all be perfect for them both. Tonight, all the moving would be done, and after Darren returned with the last load, the two of them would have pizza together, which was Darren's idea.

Around seven-thirty that evening, Darren returned from the final run. He could see a fire burning in the fireplace and the other light on in the house was coming from the master bedroom.

"I'm back, babe," he hollered when he walked in the door. "I have a loaded pizza. Did you pick a movie?"

He put the food items on the dining room table and removed his coat. "Avery? Where are you? I'm back!"

Darren looked in the kitchen, peeked out through the door leading to the garage, checked the bathroom, and finally made his way down the hall to their room. When he opened the door, there was Avery, sitting up on the bed with pillows propped behind her back. She wore a white silk gown, had candles lit all around, and her hair was brushed and styled to perfection.

"Hello, love," Avery said softly, smiling at him, and he noticed.

"I take it you have some pretty big plans for tonight, Dear." Darren grinned.

She nodded, then gestured with her right hand to the bed. "I have something for you."

Darren walked to the foot of the bed and sat on the edge. "What's this?"

"You'll have to come find out." The tone of her voice excited him, his heart began to beat so hard he thought he might pass out.

"Avery, I love you."

She didn't answer, she just stared at his face smiling and said, "Get over here."

R.W.K. Clark

CHAPTER 4

Two weeks later.

Elliot Keller sat rigidly on his bunk, waiting to be called out of the cell for his overnight laundry work detail. His face was devoid of expression, his hands resting calmly in his lap. His mind, however, was not still. It was focusing solely on the night that lay before him, for it would consist of much more than washing, drying, folding, and signing for worthless deliveries.

"Keller!"

Without hesitation, he moved forward and stopped dead before the door as it slid open on its track, culminating in a metallic bang as it reached the end. Keller stepped forward and took the same position, hands clasped behind his back, in the corridor; the door reversed, closed, and slammed into place behind him once again. Soon, he was making his way up the corridor toward the metal door at the end, ignoring the loud, obnoxious snores coming from the other men on M Corridor. He had far more important things complicating his mind right then.

The door popped, and Keller jerked it open so he could pass through. As it slammed shut behind him, a night-shift correctional officer named Kolchak rounded the corner, pulling his black latex gloves taut against his fingers. Keller smiled on the inside, but maintained his stoic façade flawlessly.

"Ready, Keller?"

Keller took the front, walking so that the corrections officer could keep his eyes on the inmate at all times from behind. With his hands still clasped behind his back per prison policy, Keller strolled at a steady, even pace in silence. It was the escorting officer who finally spoke first.

"From what I hear, you've taken to night-shift laundry like a fish to water," Kolchak remarked in a friendly, conversational tone. "I gotta say, I'm glad to hear it. I thought you would be the perfect man for the job, the way you keep to yourself and all, you know?"

"Thank you for that, Officer Kolchak."

The middle-aged man cleared his throat lightly. "No problem. Once you're in a place like this, that's punishment enough, I say. Might as well go on and try to live out your life the best you can. I know that a lot of people think that, well, you ought to be dead and all, but I figure the Man upstairs would have made that happen if that was what he wanted. I know you ain't a praying man, but you know what I mean, right Keller?"

"Yes, sir. I surely do." He couldn't help but laugh to himself: what a joke. The only gods on this planet were the men who stood up and made the things happen that they wanted to. Most of them were politicians, but the rest of them were like him. Yes, he was a god, all right.

The men continued to walk, with Kolchak humming a slight tune as they went. As far as corrections officers went, Keller thought this one was one of the better ones, just here to do his job, with no personal agendas, politics, or ulterior motives. At that moment, the inmate found himself relieved that this corrections officer would not be the one looking in on him periodically, or doing the task of monitoring late-night delivery drop-offs. This one didn't deserve what was to come, but there are those who did.

"So, sir, who's going to be my stop-in supervisor tonight, do you know?" Keller's voice was polite and respectful, just the way it ought to be. This was the perfect way to keep up a smooth rapport with officers like Kolchak; as long as you did what you were supposed to, they continued to treat you like a human being.

Even if you weren't a human being at all.

"Hmm, lemme see…" The corrections officer had to think about it. "Jacobs, I'm pretty sure. Yeah, that's right… Jacobs."

Kolchak said the man's name as if it left a taste in his mouth, and out of the corner of Keller's eyes, he saw the corrections officer crinkle his nose with distaste. A partial smile curled over Keller's lips. "Jacobs. That makes for an easy night's work. Glad it's him."

"Yeah, he's all right, I s'pose." Kolchak didn't sound too sure.

Keller hated Jacobs, it was as simple as that, and when he had been working up his plan for tonight, it was precisely Jacobs who he hoped would be his stop-in super for the shift. The guy was smug, arrogant, and the biggest jerk on Earth. One time when he stopped in during the night, Keller was doing paperwork at the desk; Jacobs snuck up behind him and shouted, right next to his ear, 'Up against the wall and drop your scrub pants, pretty boy! We've had our eye on you!' It scared the heck out of Keller. The first time he did it, Keller jumped up swinging, thinking it was some inmates from the block units, and he wasn't about to be turned out. That wasn't the case, though.

It had been Jacobs. He caught Keller's swinging arms and proceeded to beat him about the stomach with his stick until Keller was a doubled-up, puking mess in a ball on the floor. The dirtball had stood over him laughing, telling him it was all in fun and to keep his murdering mouth shut. He said that Keller better buck up, because this was how things were done in night laundry, and he told him again that it was all in fun. Then he left Keller in his own vomit, laughing all the way out the door to the laundry sally port.

Yes, Jacobs would do; Jacobs would do just fine.

"Well, Keller, here we are."

Kolchak waved to the corrections officer in the Reception & Delivery control center.

The door buzzed, and Keller entered ahead of the officer. Turning around, he thanked the man standing at the door, who also bid him a good night. Then, he turned to the inmate he was relieving who had two softcover paperbacks in his hands; obviously, this one had done a lot of work during his shift, Keller thought sarcastically. The inmate left without so much as a spit to his feet.

"Good riddance."

Making his way to the desk to see the daily logs, Keller found himself thinking about Jacobs. The man would stop in any second to do his first check; Keller planned to wait until after the midnight supply delivery to act. Once the boxes of supplies were secured in the area, Jacobs would take a final look around, and then Keller would make his move.

Picking up his clipboard to see exactly what that inmate had and hadn't done, Keller began to go about his night as if everything were as normal as a sunny day. He even hummed to himself as he stood with his rear end propped against the edge of the big oak desk, facing the sally port and the corrections officer entrance next to it. Any second, that jerk Jacobs would come through the door, spouting his baloney, and Keller would react as he always did, with a smirk and a nod, or a 'yes sir,' if the situation warranted. He would continue to do that for the next few hours, but soon enough, his responses and attitudes would make a drastic change, believe that.

As if on cue, the corrections officer entrance door buzzed loudly. Jacobs slammed his way inside, and Keller could immediately tell that the man was on the outs. He had a sneer on his face, and he appeared to be a bit flushed, a look that didn't complement his bright-red hair.

"Keller! I see you're going at it… good! I don't want any hassles tonight. If I get any, you can kiss this job goodbye right on the rear. I have my own problems to worry about without having to worry about you too."

Jacobs simply stood in the doorway, letting the cold air and large flakes of snow blow inside. Keller stood still, clipboard in hand and page half-turned.

The only thing he had moved since the man presented himself were his eyes, and now they held Jacobs mean gaze unflinchingly.

"Well?" Jacobs was beginning to raise his voice.

"Yes sir."

The corrections officer flinched almost unnoticeably at the stillness in Keller's voice and the lack of reaction he showed at the man's words. As if he realized that he had flinched, Jacobs glanced over his shoulder at the corrections officer tower outside, then stepped through the door and let it slam shut behind him. Strolling over to Keller, he stopped in front of him and put his face directly into that of the inmate's. Keller set the clipboard on the desk without even realizing what he was doing, intent on keeping eyes with the bully of a correctional officer that stood before him. Maybe he wouldn't be waiting until two after all. This guy was going to jack his plans all up, and he wasn't having it.

Suddenly, the intercom buzzed to life; both men nearly jumped out of their skin.

"The soap and toiletries delivery is here!"

Jacobs jerked his head to the right. "Now?"

"Yep. Early because of the coming storm!"

"Pop the sally! Let's get this over with!" Jacobs said after a brief pause. He turned back to Keller and smiled. "Aren't you the lucky one."

Keller simply stared back at him. "I suppose I am, sir."

Jacobs' smile faltered once again, then he muttered in a low voice, "Let's get this over with."

Keller made the guy nervous, he knew. He was also aware that was the main reason that the young ginger-haired punk treated him like he did. Sure, he was rude to the others, but when it came to Keller, Jacobs became a special kind of menace. It was almost as if he would rape Keller if given the opportunity. Keller would love to give him the opportunity, because he'd flip the script on the punk so fast the guy would think he woke up in a very painful alternate universe.

For the next hour, Keller tolerated the insolent man the best he could while he unloaded boxes of state manufactured toiletry products. Jacobs held the clipboard, making sure the order had been properly filled while the truck driver sat in the cab of the truck. He was a lazy loser, and though he put on good appearances when it came to looking like he was hands-on work-wise, he was actually just below a bonbon eating fatty who was addicted to 'As the World Turns.'

It was during that time, and while thinking over all those thoughts, that Keller realized that the time to act was at hand.

"Wait, I put the wrong number of boxes of toilet paper here," Jacobs said. "You said fifteen hundred-count boxes, right, Keller?"

"Fifteen, right." He pretended to recount with a pointed finger, but his eyes were on Jacobs' back, and Keller was well aware of the level of distraction the man had sunk into.

Jacobs turned his back on Keller right then to set the clipboard on the desk to erase and correct. He also put his oversized black flashlight on the desk chair, forgotten, while he did the task. It took Keller absolutely no time to think it through; it was perfect. If Keller had one thing going for him, it was the speed in which he was able to think and move.

Keller snatched up the flashlight so fast that his movements were nothing more than a blur and a shadow to the naked eye. With a single powerful overhand swing, he smashed Jacobs in the head with the large end of it, and the man instantly crumpled to the floor, lifeless but for a few random twitches here and there. Keller looked at him with a smile, briefly, before smashing him in the head again, and again, and yet again. Blood was pooling all over the concrete floor beneath his head, threatening to hypnotize Keller and distract him from the goal. If he had his way, he would have sodomized the loser right then and there.

At last, Keller stood back, swept his long, sweaty black hair from his eyes, and smiled down at the man. His head was now nothing more than a bloody pulp with a small spot of brain pulsating grotesquely in one spot; the pulses were visibly slowing down, and Keller was tempted to sit and watch until they stopped completely, but now was not the time. Tossing the flashlight on the floor, he grabbed the corrections officer's gun and took it out of its holster. He made sure the safety was off, then ran over to the rear of the truck that was still sticking through the sally port. He gave the back a kick.

"Hey, we need you in here!" he yelled to the driver. "These orders are all messed up, man!"

There was no response, but he heard the man get out of the truck and slam the door. In seconds, the corrections officer entrance was popping open, and the driver was coming inside. Keller, who was hidden just inside, let the door slam, then hustled the driver against the wall forcefully, the gun to his head.

"Take off your clothes," he growled.

The driver began to whimper immediately. "Don't... please. I have– "

"Shut up and take off your clothes!"

It took the man less than a minute to shed everything but his underwear. He was shivering from both the cold and his own fear as he tossed the items on top of a box of toilet paper as Keller directed him. Turning to Keller expectantly, he acted as if he was going to wait for his next instructions, but there were to be none. Keller smiled at him, pushed him against the wall, and smashed the butt of the gun in to his head. The young man dropped to his knees, then fell over dead. Keller looked him over; there was no pulsating bits of brain this time. Boring, he thought.

Now it was time to dress. First, he pulled his hair back into a makeshift bun using a rubber band from the desk drawer; if anything gave him away it would be his long black hair. Next, he put on the driver's uniform, including his hat, making sure any stragglers from his black tresses were tucked up inside. He had given himself a good shave that day, and in the shadowy lighting, he doubted that the corrections officers would see his face at all. He wasn't worried; he was driving out of there in minutes.

Keller lowered the door on the back of the truck, secured it, then went to the corrections officer door and pressed the button. "It's just Justin, the driver" he said into the box after they answered him. "They thought they were short TP, but we're good."

Without any suspicion or further questions, the door buzzed. Keller stepped out and went around to the driver's side of the truck, jumped in, and pulled out. In his rearview mirror, he watched as the sally port door was lowered by the corrections officer in the Reception & Delivery control center. Keller smiled, nodded, and gave a partial salute to the man running the show in the control center as he passed by and drove through the checkpoint.

In seconds, Elliot Keller was driving down the highway through the fresh falling snow, away from the prison and out of sight.

CHAPTER 5

"Hey, babe! Got the broken heater in that second cabin up and running like a top. You might wanna get in there and give it a good refreshing, never know what will happen with this second storm going on."

Donna looked up from the very last of the file work she had been pounding away at. It had taken her all of two weeks to scan all of the remaining old files from the cabin resort into the new system, making sure they were all in properly labeled folders and in some kind of discernable order. It was a bummer this project had consisted of so much work; it was highly likely that they would never need to get anything out of the files in the future.

"I'm on my last stack here, Rick," she said, beaming as her husband removed his coat and headed for the coffee pot. "When I'm finished, I'll get to cabin two. I doubt anyone will be stopping or demanding that specific cabin in the next fifteen minutes. Besides, even if they did, we do have others we could rent while I get that one back in shape. Sometimes you think the goofiest thoughts, I swear."

Rick rubbed his hands together, then grabbed the carafe of coffee and poured a steaming hot cup. "That's fine; by the time you take your little butt over there, the cabin will be nice and warm. It smells musty, though, so I figure you'll wanna dust and change the linens and towels. I don't think we've rented it out in a while, have we?"

"No. I'll give it a good going over. Now, let me finish this."

Donna went back to the files, and Rick, who had managed to drain the last cup of coffee, set about making another pot. The couple worked in near silence, the only sound being the scanning of old paperwork and the percolation of the coffee pot. Rick stood before it like an impatient child who just had a bubble gum machine steal all of his change. His fingers tapped impatiently against the counter as the chills from the frigid outside air continued to course uncomfortably through his body. He was also tapping his foot, as though the extra movement would intimidate the ancient coffeemaker into speeding things up a bit.

"This has got to be the slowest pot in the free world," he muttered. "You know, Donna, if things pick up, even in the slightest this year, our lobby and the full continental breakfast will be going through an overhaul before the new season begins. New coffee pot, some furniture that doesn't look like it came out of the Bates Motel, and maybe even an expansion, a kitchen, so we can begin to serve meals on grounds."

"Rick," she replied with a shake of her head, "I know the thing seems slow to you, but it does spit out a pot in less than a minute. But, okay, I'll concede: if things pick up, we'll get a brand new shiny one just for your satisfaction."

Finishing the very last of the files, Donna returned them to the old box from which they came, then stood, stretched, and made her way to her coat. She grabbed the key to cabin two, tucked it into her pocket, and went into the back housekeeping area where all of the sheets, soaps, toilet papers, and other complementary bathroom items were kept. Donna loaded a cart with the things she would need for cleaning and spiffing up the cabin, pecked her husband on the cheek, and made her way out of the office, across the lot, and to cabin two.

Rick took Donna's seat behind the desk; after all, it was the best seat in the 'house,' enabling anyone who sat behind it to see all who entered and exited from the lot. Sure, there was property access from the lake in the back, but at this point in the winter storm, it would be not just difficult but impossible to reach the small beaches on the lake which were directly behind the cabin resort itself. It would take a special kind of man, to endure the frigid, murderous waters at this point in the game. So, needless to say, Rick kept his eyes on the office doors, windows, and parking lots.

∞

The man stepped out from a dense thicket of bushes. He was wearing a brown delivery suit, and his face was partially covered with a ski mask. It was colder than sin out there, but he was pretty sure he had found a safe haven where he would be comfortable until the storm eased up, and he could continue his route to Rocky Mount. Nothing like traveling to make one's heart full.

He approached the cluster of cabins. Through the distance, he could see a pretty woman pushing a cart across the parking lot. A man about the same age was sitting near a big picture window.

Yes, this was more than perfect.

∞

It didn't take long before something got Rick's attention out of the corner of his eye: a man in what appeared to be a brown delivery suit of some sort was entering the lot, and he was on foot. He had something like a thick black scarf covering the lower part of his face; the item seemed matted with ice and snow, at least from what he could see from inside the office. He also wore what appeared to be a delivery man's hat, and it had a nice pile of snow resting on top. Rick rose and made his way to the door to open it for the stranger; hopefully, the man wanted a cabin, but if nothing else, Rick could at least bring him inside and warm him up with a stout cup of java. Surely the stranger would appreciate that.

As soon as the door was opened, a frigid gust of air rushed in, blowing snow and wetness in behind it. The man quickly entered, and Rick closed the door then turned to him, looking him up and down and trying to read him by his outward appearance. It was strange, but he seemed to get a vibe from the stranger that was off, a bit uncomfortable. The guy hadn't even said a word, so what was all this apprehension about?

"What seems to be the problem, sir?" He asked politely. "Are you needing to rent a cabin? Did your vehicle break down or get stuck somewhere?"

The stranger shivered violently and shook his head in response to both questions. "Umm-m, could I please just have a cup of coffee for now, please? I sort of need to get my wits about me, you know. It's so cold out there I could barely breathe."

Rick jumped into action. "Oh, yeah, man. Sure thing. Do you take it black?"

"As the night," the man replied.

As Rick poured the shivering man a large cup of coffee, his curiosity got the best of him, and he repeated his question. "Did your vehicle break down somewhere down the main road? I mean, not to impose, but if that's the case, we have a dependable winter tow service here in Thompson Trails that would be more than willing to help you, if that's the case. The sheriff has a tow plow, and he takes great pleasure in putting that beast to use."

He handed the coffee to the stranger, who still had yet to remove the partial ski mask he was wearing, which was covering most of his face, except for his eyes. He sipped the coffee right through the slit in his mask, sopping it with the hot liquid. Rick supposed he didn't mind; after all, the hot coffee would likely warm his lips for a bit before he decided to hit the road once again, if it didn't sear his flesh off, first.

"So, you rent these cabins out, huh?" the man asked.

Rick leaned against the main desk with his elbow and sipped his own java. "Yeah, but I have to admit, we really don't expect to get any guests during this particular storm. We had a doozy of a storm two weeks ago." All at once, Rick got the overwhelming feeling that this was the last man in the world he wanted to rent to.

The man held his black eyes on Rick's hazel ones, never shifting his gaze, staring and seemingly reading the innermost parts of his mind, delving into his most personal thoughts. A chill came over the young resort owner, and he tried, unsuccessfully, to shake it off. This guy was definitely off, and the heebie-jeebies he was sending in Rick's direction were enough to make him both nauseous and defensive all at the same time. The bottom line was that the more Rick Welk stood with the stranger in the lobby of the Virginia Trailhead Cabins, the more he felt like he wanted to crawl out of there and run screaming. He glanced at Donna's empty chair and was glad she had headed to the cabin.

"So, Mr. -" he began.

The stranger smirked. "Derringer. Elias Derringer."

"So, Mr. Derringer, were you interested in one of the cabins for the week?" Rick was hoping not, deep down in his gut. One guy's money wasn't going to make or break them in the slightest.

Derringer took a long slug of the slowly cooling coffee and shrugged. "I'm not quite sure. They look pretty quaint, but I'd rather get a look at one of them."

"Well, you head on outside. My wife is cleaning one of them, so I'll grab my coat, and meet you out there so you can see what we have to offer." With that, Rick went into the men's room, and Elias Derringer wasted no time in leaving the resort lobby and heading to the one cabin with a cart parked in front of it: cabin two.

Rick stood at the head draining his bladder. His mind turned to the stranger... what was his name? Derringer. Elias Derringer. Something was off about the man, something that Rick couldn't quite put his finger on. The guy, while seemingly pleasant enough, had shifty eyes, and the pleasant tone of his voice didn't match his disposition. Suddenly, Rick's stomach got a bit upset. Had he really just sent that stranger ahead of him to cabin two, alone, to see the cabin while his wife was the only one in there? Rick began to furiously shake, it seemed urgent all of a sudden that he get out to that cabin and make sure that all was well. Something inside of him said he had just done one of the dumbest things he had ever done in his life.

He rushed from the bathroom, grabbing his coat, and ran out the office door. Derringer was nowhere in sight; obviously, he was already in the cabin with Donna. The door to cabin two was slightly open, and the lights from inside were casting a wedge of illumination over the snow. Every now and then he could see the shadow of either Donna or the stranger as it passed through the light stream. Rick picked up his step, and now he was almost jogging through the rapidly piling snow on the lot.

As he approached, he could hear Derringer speaking to Donna.

"So, I see it's pretty dead right now," he was saying. "Is that because of the weather, or are y'all dead around here most of the time, pretty lady?"

Donna chuckled, but the nervousness in her voice was almost tangible. "Um, just the storm, I'm pretty sure. We're busy most all the time." She paused. "Where did you say my husband is?"

"Oh, just using the facilities, ma'am." The man laughed, but there was something a bit sinister to the sound. "You must get pretty lonely out here, what, with your husband leaving all the hard stuff to you."

"No, he does all the hard work," she replied pleasantly, burying her concern and nervousness. "I just pick up the slack around here and handle the paperwork."

Rick immediately picked up on the change in the man's voice; it had now taken on a flirtatious tone, but there was an underflow of dirtiness to it, as though the thoughts in his mind weren't matching the concern that he was feigning. Nauseous, he felt the overwhelming need to get this guy off the property. Rick took hold of the cabin door, swung it open, and planted a tight-lipped smile on his face.

"So, Mr. Derringer… what do you think of the cabin?" he asked. His voice bordered on rude now; he didn't want Elias Derringer renting a cabin, or anything else for that matter. The guy's aura was filthy, and its blackness was almost something he could see and touch.

Both Donna and the stranger were startled by his sudden appearance, though he noted clearly that his wife looked relieved to see him. Derringer, on the other hand, looked more amused than anything. Rick's belly gave another uneasy lurch. Was this guy playing some kind of game, or was Rick over-reacting, as Donna often said he did?

Derringer smirked. "Not bad; not bad at all. As a matter of fact, pretty cozy, considering all things. You two have sure managed to make a nice little getaway spot here for passers-through, I have to say." The man looked at Donna and gave her a wink; her face turned red, and even a little green around the gills. The stranger was managing to make her very uncomfortable indeed. She turned away from him and went into the bathroom with a can of cleanser and a toilet brush.

"So," Rick continued, his eyes still on his wife protectively. "Are you interested in renting, or not." His smile was tight, and his hospitality had reached its end.

Derringer began to pace around the cabin once again, this time poking his head into the bathroom, the small closet, and even kneeling to look under the bed. "How much for the night?"

Rick wanted to laugh. "For the night? But we just rent by the week. After all, this is the Virginia Trailhead Cabins; most guests make a time of it. It's not a roadside inn, you know. A week is two-fifty, full facility access, including canoes and lake use."

"You aren't willing to rent to me for a single night?" Derringer asked, an edge to his voice. "Even with the storm and all? I mean, I ran into some bad luck in Donneley's Pass; got robbed, you know. Could use a shower and a place to lay my head."

Rick shook his head. "Sorry, man. A week only." He did not want the so-and-so there for another second.

Out of the blue, Derringer broke out into a sick, dangerous laugh, as though Rick had just cracked the funniest joke of all time. Both Donna and Rick just stared at him as the laughter ran its course, glancing at each other uneasily out of the corner of their eyes, half-smiles on their faces to appear polite.

"Nah, I think I'll have to pass; these are a little too rich for my taste, ya see."

Rick nodded. "Well, I'm sorry to hear that, Mr...."

"Derringer," the man replied through gritted teeth, with a sneer and a glare in Rick's direction.

Rick nodded pleasantly and smiled with relief. "Yes, Derringer. My apologies. Well, as you can see, the missus and I have to finish up the loose ends in this cabin. You know, if you head up the main highway, the sheriff's office is about a half-mile up on the right, and old Sheriff Brown and his deputy are always more than willing to help out when it comes to taking those down on their luck to safer waters. He even gives out vouchers to passers-through for the local hotel up in the next town, probably drive you there, too. You should really head that way. If you want, I'll give him a call for you, and I'm sure he'll pick you up and take you that way."

Derringer maintained his odd grin and continued to look around the cabin covetously. "Nah. I'll hike, I do believe. This is a pretty small homestead, this Thompson Trails. I think I'll be just fine. Well, now, folks. Thank you for the hospitality, but I do believe I'll be on my way."

Relief flooded Rick's body. "Well, sure was nice to meet you. Hope you don't hit the worst of the storm that's coming."

Derringer stopped at the door and turned back to both of them, offering Donna one more wink. "Oh, I do believe that all of us are going to be getting the worst of the storm that's coming, Mr. Welk. The worst of it, in the worst kind of way."

With that, Elias Derringer left cabin two, slamming the door shut behind him. When Rick peeked out the flowered curtains, he saw Derringer heading for the entrance to the lot, and he breathed a sigh of relief.

"What a weirdo," he muttered under his breath.

Donna went back to changing the sheets on the bed. "Well, I don't know, dear. Everyone is weird in their own way. He was pleasant enough to me."

"The look on your face said differently, Hun," he replied in disbelief. "I saw your eyes, and I know you heard how he spoke and acted. Something was wrong with that guy."

She shrugged and ignored him. It really didn't matter; the stranger was gone now. His odd behavior was no longer the concern of Rick and Donna Welk.

R.W.K. Clark

CHAPTER 6

The snow, even though the flakes were huge and falling peacefully, was coming down in great torrents. The wind blew ferociously, whistling here and there without a care, and the six o'clock evening news was warning all residents and travelers in the area to find and maintain shelter immediately. It didn't look as if this one was going to pass too soon at all. The fascinating thing about it all was that it seemed it was never going to end.

Well, this is the way it goes... the uncertainty, the pain, and the doubt, all of it. The weather was frigid, and the icy gusts of wind made it even worse. Derringer kept his head down against its onslaught. He trudged through the rapidly piling snow and thought about the couple back at the cabin resort. He could tell that the husband had been on to him. Maybe he had no idea what Derringer was really all about, but he could tell by the look in the man's eyes that the guy was super-uncomfortable in his presence, and he should be.

Elias Derringer had considered taking that Donna Welk lady and showing her a trick or two while they were talking in the cabin. As a matter of fact, he hadn't really even heard a word the pleasant blond had said to him; he had been too busy wondering what her blood would feel like dripping from his fingers, or how she felt from the inside, with his brutal fist. But then, alas, the mister had come charging across the lot, and his attitude had changed drastically from the way it had been in the office.

Derringer shrugged against the cold, then paused briefly to adjust his foot a bit in his prison issue boots. The corrections officer Jacobs' gun was tucked away neatly in there, but it was pretty uncomfortable, not to mention the fact that it was colder than a witch's tit in a steel bra. He had almost left it in the delivery truck when he sent it careening down the side of a steep embankment about three miles back, but then thought better of it. There was nothing better than to have fun and games with a large handgun, especially when it came to the fun and games he liked to have with the female of the species. It was his full intent to indulge himself, so keeping the weapon was a given.

His mind went back to the Welks; yes, he would return there, and he would have his fun. He would christen every cabin at that resort with the blood of that couple, and he would stretch out his little games for as long as possible. He wasn't fooling himself; he would be caught eventually. There were all-points bulletins out on him all over the state of Virginia, and all surrounding states as well. Derringer's appearance made him stand out in a crowd, his long, scraggly black hair was a dead giveaway. He made sure it was tucked out of sight under the hat, and he figured he would be safe from capture for a while anyway. It really didn't matter though; if he thought he was at risk for apprehension, he'd blow out the brains of anyone threatening his little adventure, and of that, he had no doubt.

Derringer noticed a small, hidden alleyway off to the side of what appeared to be an old abandoned feed store. With a quick glance around at the deserted street, he ducked into the alley and crouched down behind a dumpster to get out of the wind. He would wait here until the sun was completely down, then he would make his way back to the cabin resort. The Welks would be in bed by then for sure, then he could get inside one of the cabins, warm up, and wait to get that pretty little blond by the throat the next morning at the first opportunity.

An hour later, Derringer was crossing the parking lot once again to Virginia Trailhead Cabins. Cabin ten had the flicker of a television light shining through the drawn curtains; this must be the Welks' quarters, he thought to himself. Making his way to the front of the office, he crouched down next to a snow-covered garbage can and tried to get warm once again. He was shivering like a leaf in a high wind, and he was even starting to feel like he was coming down with something; the urge to cough was overwhelming.

After about ten minutes of fighting the cough, Derringer lost control. He began to hack and choke in earnest, and his body was so wracked with the coughs that he didn't see or hear Rick Welk open the door to the cabin and look out at him. Derringer just continued to cough.

"What are you doing back here?"

Rick's voice startled the escapee. He swung his head, thinking fast while he tried to stop the choking. He felt fury building up inside of him at the self-righteous prick standing there, looking at him as if he were a pile of dog excrement that hadn't been cleaned up.

"Um, I'm sorry sir," he said, trying to sound as cold and miserable as possible. "I just needed to warm up, just for a second; I think I got turned around in the storm somehow. Isn't it possible I could do some work for you for a cabin for the night?"

Rick stared at him, his stomach giving a lurch of warning. He thought about the request; it seemed innocent enough. But whatever was making him uneasy about Elias Derringer was what he was going to base his decision on. Rick had always been one to follow his gut, and he wasn't about to deviate from that habit now.

"Look, man, I'm really sorry," he replied, trying to be kind, but with an edge to his voice. "You simply need to go. I'm sure if you head to the sheriff's station, he would put you up for the night."

Derringer sneered. "You think so, huh?"

Rick just stared at him; something was off, so he backed up into the cabin and closed the door slightly. "Yeah. Just head left on the highway, and it's about half a mile up."

"Heck," Derringer muttered as he stood and headed off again. He'd be back; this guy had better know it.

Rick watched him walk away until he turned out of sight on the highway, then he closed the cabin door and locked it. "I'm calling Sheriff Brown. That same weirdo was out there under the awning, next to the garbage can. Maybe they can put him up in the jail."

"But he really hasn't done anything wrong, has he Dear?" Donna asked, but she didn't sound convinced about the man's innocence.

Rick shook his head adamantly and picked up the phone. "I don't care if he's the son of Mother Teresa; I'm calling Bob."

Donna didn't say a word to disagree while Rick dialed Bob Brown's office. He filled him in on the vagrant, and on the discomfort the guy made him feel. Bob Brown reassured Rick that he would head out right then and track down the guy, then told him to hit the hay, keep warm, and sleep well.

Hanging up the phone, Rick did just as his friend suggested, and in no time at all, he and Donna were both snoring lightly, all thoughts of the odd man out of their minds and dreams.

∞

Sheriff Bob Brown sat bundled up in the pickup plow, a magnetic cop light on the dashboard turned to the off position, with the heater and defrost set to high. He was parked facing the direction of the cabin resort, waiting for any sign of the stranger Rick had reported, and as he watched, he hummed along to a country song telling him how mama had tried to raise him better. He wished that the guy would show his face; Bob wanted to get home to his sweet Rosie and some warm apple pie.

It didn't take the man long to come into view, even in the near-blizzard conditions. Before long, the tall shadow of the man could be seen struggling through the snow as he made his way toward the sheriff. The drifting snow was causing him to stagger a bit, and the high winds didn't help matters, either. Bob noticed that he was wearing a partial face mask, like something skiers wore; it was probably his best clothing choice of the day, all things considered.

Brown watched, his eyes squinted in the darkness, as he reached for the spotlight on his car door. He almost instantly changed his mind, though; he didn't know this guy, and for all he knew, the spotlight would freak him out and send him into some kind of tizzy. Instead, Brown turned on the fog lamps so as to not blind the man, then slowly began to drive in the stranger's direction. The snow was getting really deep, he thought briefly. Everyone would be using their snowmobiles by morning. He found himself thankful over and over that he had invested in this great big rig.

Brown continued forward at a snail's pace, taking note that the man didn't slow or stop at his approach. Instead, he continued to walk an even pace in the calf-high snow, his hands in his pockets and his head covered with a hat. The sheriff pulled up next to the man, stopped the truck, and rolled down the passenger side window.

"Excuse me," he hollered to the stranger. "I'm the sheriff here in Thompson Trails. Is there any way I can help you?"

Brown squinted at him in the darkness, looking for any reaction or response, but the guy just acted like he didn't hear or see him. Sure, the wind was blowing good, Bob Brown thought, but he was practically pulled right up next to the guy. The sheriff sat there waiting, but the guy continued to walk.

Brown grabbed his bull horn. "Excuse me, sir! I'm Sheriff Bob Brown. Could I have your attention please?"

All at once, as if on cue, the stranger stopped dead in his tracks. He kept his head down, not turning around, and his hands were still buried in his pockets. Bob clucked his tongue, shook his head, and put the vehicle in park, rolling up the passenger side window as he went. Why did all the strange so-and-so's in the world have to make each and every single thing so difficult?

Brown unclipped his gun at his side and got out of the truck, hand securely on his pistol. Slowly, he walked around to the back, where the man was standing, right at the bumper of the truck. Brown approached him slowly, his hand still on his gun.

"It's mighty cold out here, sir," he said kindly. "You have to be about frozen by now. Is there anything I can do to help you?"

When he received no reply, he continued. "Boy, you came to town at the wrong time. Nobody's really taking borders, you know. I guess you must have tried down at the cabins, but even they decided to shut in for the night." He paused again; for some reason or other, Bob Brown felt a bit uncomfortable. The guy just didn't act like anyone who simply needed help. As a matter of fact, he acted like there was something in his head that wasn't too pleasant at all.

"I'm going to have to ask you for some identification, sir." Bob tightened his grip on his gun.

Finally, the stranger turned in his direction and offered a pleasant smile that Bob could only identify through the eyeholes of the half-mask.

"I ain't got none, sir. See, that's the problem: I was robbed down at Donneley's Pass at the truck stop. All my money, license, everything gone. I was just trying to make my way as far as I could 'til I finally get home safe."

"Where you from?" Brown began to relax a tad now; the guy seemed more and more harmless with each passing second. Maybe it was just the darkness and the wind that made the man seem so eerie.

The stranger took a deep breath. "Rocky Mount."

Brown took a good look around. The streets were completely dead and snow-covered; it was ridiculous to keep this guy standing out in the middle of the crazy snow. The least he could do was let the guy warm up and help him figure something out.

"Hey, if you wanna climb in the truck, we could get you warmed up, and we'll run your name, make sure you're clear. If you're good to go, why, we'll just put you up in our one-cell pokey for the night, free of charge. Then, in the morning, we can call down to the train station in Donneley's Pass, get you a ticket, and I can run you on the snowmobile to catch the train to Rocky Mount. How's that sound to you?"

Derringer thought about it for a fraction of a second. "Sounds wonderful to me. I can't thank you enough."

In minutes, the two men were seated, in the pickup plow, contrary to state law and local policy. Derringer had his gloves off and was rubbing his hands together in front of the heater vent. Sheriff Brown poured the stranger a steaming cup of java from his thermos, then used an old styrofoam cup for himself. Grabbing his notebook and pen, the cop decided to get down to business.

"I'll need your name, date of birth, and social security number, please, sir."

The man gave a shiver as the heat began to settle into his bones. "Derringer. Elias Derringer. Birth date June sixth of sixty-nine."

Brown scratched at the notepad furiously. "Social?"

Derringer smiled on the inside. He had thought of this before, and he had used the name Elias Derringer, the man's birth date, and his social security number on several occasions, all successfully. Elias was his cousin on his mother's side. He was locked up in a private institution that his rich mother paid for, safe from the public eye and all scrutiny. The idiot had never been in trouble a day in his life; he could barely wipe his own bum.

More scribbling, then Sheriff Brown took the handset to his police radio and called into the station. "Hey, Darren, this is Bob here. I got this half-frozen man with me. I need you to run his information right quick."

"Shoot," a younger voice replied.

Brown gave the information over the radio, then refilled both of their coffee cups. "So, you're from Rocky Mount, eh?"

"Yeah, but I ain't had much opportunity to pass through in a while. Most of my relatives are fairly well-off; they live in Roanoke. But I have some old friends I stop in and see in the Mount. Why?" Derringer looked out of the corner of his eye at the cop. "You know anyone from there?"

"Nah. Thompson Trails folk are born here, they live here, and mostly they die here, too. The only time I ever leave is to take the wife to her medical appointments at the Pass." Both men gave a chuckle at that one.

The radio crackled loudly. "Hey, Bob. Looks like Mr. Derringer's clean as a whistle."

"Thank you, Darren," the sheriff replied. "Seems he had a touch of trouble down in Donneley's Pass; got robbed but good. We're gonna put him in the cell for the night, and in the morning, we'll get him a ticket to Rocky Mount out of the town fund. Why don't you go ahead and get it ready."

"Yes, sir."

With the radio conversation over, Brown turned to Derringer. "So, you ready to get a warm shower and some sleep? We ain't got much food, maybe a couple of microwave burritos in the fridge, and I think there might be a donut or two... hope that will do ya."

Derringer smiled slyly to himself. "That would be just perfect, sir. Once again, I can't thank you enough."

As they whipped a u-turn to head back to the station, Derringer thought, "Oh, but I'm sure I'll find a way to repay your kindness, Sheriff Brown."

CHAPTER 7

"Well, howdy Boss!" Deputy Darren Rush's voice seemed to boom inside the small main office in the brick building that served as both Thompson Trails city hall and jail. The man was young, no more than twenty-five, and he had a bright red jarhead haircut that seemed to stand straight up. He was tall and thin, Derringer could easily tell, even though the kid was sitting down with his legs reclined on the desk. Probably six-two, but he couldn't have weighed much more than a buck-eighty.

Sheriff Brown grunted. "Howdy. Smells good in here. Bet this was the first real cleaning this place has had in a year." He turned to Derringer. "In case you hadn't guessed already, we really don't get many overnighters here in Thompson Trails, at least when it comes to the jail. Mostly, it's here for appearance sake." The sheriff gave a big belly laugh at his own joke.

Darren stood and held out his hand to Derringer. "I'm Deputy Rush; nice to make your acquaintance. You can call me Darren if you like."

"Likewise. I'm Elias... Elias Derringer."

Rush gestured around the musty, dusty room, which had two desks piled high with files, leaving just enough room for feet to rest. "I know it ain't much, but the shower works and the blankets are warm."

Derringer forced a pleasant smile. "Much obliged."

Darren then fetched a neatly folded towel, washcloth, toothbrush, and bar of soap. "Ain't got no paste, either. Sorry. The shower is right around the corner when you're ready. Oh, and I put a pair of old blue scrubs for you to sleep in."

"Thank you."

Derringer gave them a nod and left for the shower area while Brown plopped down and gave his own feet a rest. Removing his glasses, he began to polish the condensation off of them, his mind on his wife Rose. He knew she was okay, safe at home in the storm, but he always kept her in the forefront of his mind. He was responsible for the pretty little lady, after all. She was his dream girl, and the love of his life.

"You ain't heard from my Rosie, have ya?" Brown asked.

Darren sat back down. "She called about fifteen minutes ago. She's going to bed, and your meatloaf is in the oven. Oh, yeah, she said there's a big ole slice of pie in there too."

"Good, because I absolutely do want that."

The two men laughed hard at that one.

Rush cleared his throat. "So, you feeling okay about this stranger, are ya?"

Brown snorted. "Why shouldn't I? Poor guy got robbed, and he's been struggling all the way from Donneley's Pass. He'd have to be one psycho to pick tonight to do any damage. The guy's harmless."

"I'll take your word for it, Boss," Rush replied. "There's hot coffee there, and a couple of donuts left over from supper that the missus bought. Otherwise, I think there might be one more beef and bean burrito in the fridge. Want me to heat it for him?"

"Perfect," Brown replied, putting his glasses back on his face. "But you'd better find out what he wants exactly first; can't be wasting food. I'll hang out for a bit, have a word with Mr. Derringer and get to know him a bit. But guess what?"

Darren Rush gave a groan. "Don't tell me: I'll be staying overnight with him, just to keep an eye on our unknown guest."

"Precisely."

The two men began to chat loosely about the storm, comparing it to the last major snow the town had seen, five-years prior. According to both of their recollections, that storm had nothing on this one. This one had been touted as a killer by the news; Thompson Trails had ended up stacking this storm on top of the last one two weeks ago.

Elias Derringer rounded the corner then. He was wearing the blue scrub pants and shirt, which appeared to be a size too large for him. His towel was draped loosely over his head, and in his arms, he carried the clothing he had been wearing. It was neatly folded, with his boots on top. His wet hair was pulled back into a loose ponytail.

Sheriff Brown jumped up. "Oh, here you go, Mr. Derringer. Let me take care of that for you." The man grabbed the dirty laundry, boots and all, and walked them over to Deputy Rush. Derringer thought about the gun he had tucked in his clean sock. It made him smile anyway.

"Darren here is going to be pulling night duty tonight, since we actually have a stayover and all. He'll need to keep himself busy, and this is a good way for him to do that. Besides, got to stay in practice for when real criminals come to town, wouldn't you say, Darren?"

The deputy laughed sarcastically as Brown put the neat stack of belongings on the only bare corner of his desk. Deputy Rush grabbed the boots and put them on the floor next to the desk, then picked up the dirty clothing and stood to his feet.

"Oh, yes, sir," he replied. "As a matter of fact, there's no time like the present. Maybe you'd see fit to hook this man up with a bite and some coffee. I'll be back."

Rush went down a small hallway and out of sight, while Bob Brown waved at the donuts and coffee. "There's also those burritos I was telling you about, Elias."

Without answering, Derringer poured a cup of straight black and grabbed a glazed donut. He took a single bite, turned to the sheriff, and leaned back against the table holding the refreshments. As he chewed, he stared the lawman in the eye, observing his every move, his eyes nothing more than narrow slits. He was always thinking ahead, especially since escaping from prison. It was best to anticipate anything from anybody.

Bob Brown stared back at him in silence, the smile he had been wearing on his face disappearing in slow motion. This was a creeper, all right. No wonder Rick Welk didn't want to deal with the guy, money or not. Most of the locals, including the Welks, would have put someone up for free in weather like this, but for some reason, Rick had refused, and that wasn't like him. As Derringer took another large bite of his donut,

Brown was pretty sure he now understood why. Suddenly, he just wanted to get out of there, and fast, but he wanted the stranger locked safely in the cell first.

"Sorry to tell you, but per state and county policy we'll have to keep the cell locked tonight while you sleep," Brown quickly explained, faking a brand-new smile. "You know, it's more for your safety than anything, what, with all the weapons. Plus, you never know when some dangerous criminal will come in here and pull something crazy. I'd sure hate to see you get hurt in a random situation like that."

"Dangerous criminals coming to Thompson Trails," Derringer muttered around his donut bite. "No, we wouldn't want that now, would we."

Brown chuckled nervously just as Rush came around the corner. "Well, they're all in the wash for you. By tomorrow, you'll be good as new, Mr. Derringer."

The man gave him nothing more than a nod in response, then shoved the last of his donut in his mouth all at once. Draining his coffee, Derringer wiped his mouth with the back of his hand and gave a cockeyed grin.

"I suppose I'm pretty beat," he said, giving an exaggerated stretch and yawn. "All that treading the snow and walking, and then those punks at the Pass. I'll bet I sleep like the dead."

Brown jumped to his feet, grabbing some magazines and handing them to the man before opening the cell and letting him in. When the door was securely locked behind Derringer, who was making himself comfortable, Brown turned to Rush.

"I need you to fetch me the files, Rush," he said, giving a sly wink to his deputy.

At first Darren looked confused, but he quickly straightened up. "Oh, yeah. I found those earlier. You wouldn't believe it! They were in the female inmate files. Come on, let's go get them. You gonna take them home and write up some fresh ones? You know, those Richmond cops called earlier complaining about that again."

"Yep," Bob replied, all business. "That's my plan."

As the two cops walked out of the room, Derringer, who was pretending to read a magazine, watched them out of the corner of his eye. They weren't on to him; the phone hadn't rung, and there was no fax machine in sight. No, he just made the sheriff nervous, that was all. This wasn't new to him because he made everyone nervous. It was one of his favorite traits about himself; he wouldn't want to be any other way.

∞

"What file are you talking about, Boss? You're not making a lick of sense!"

Bob Brown and Darren Rush were standing in the back-file room, waving dust around to keep it out of their faces. Darren had already sneezed more than once, so the sheriff was trying to be patient and wait for him to get it together.

"It's really nothing big," he said. "The guy just gave me a bit of the creeps; I'm ready to go home. Look, I know the state cleared him, but just practice the strictest of procedures, okay? You never know who you got in a place like this. More than likely it's nothing; he's just cold, tired, and hungry, and I can say the same for myself."

"Got it, Boss."

Brown continued. "Now, first thing in the morning, I'll call and buy him a train ticket to Rocky Mount myself. Then, you take him most likely on the snowmobile to catch the train in Donneley's Pass; maybe he'll even spot those people who ripped him off. Now, that's the plan. I want this guy out of Thompson Trails before my gut proves me right, just like it always does."

Brown gave a firm slap to Rush's shoulder, smiled grimly, and continued. "Not that I think anything is going to happen, mind you. More than likely the storm has me all paranoid and up in arms. All I'm saying is exercise precaution; he's a stranger in these parts. Clean record or not, we always need to keep on the side of caution, son. Don't be overly suspicious with him, or rude, but don't get too close, either. I mean, who really ventures out on foot in this weather when they get mugged? No one."

Rush nodded soberly. "Yes, sir. Anything you say."

"All right." Bob grabbed an empty file folder, tucked a couple of blank sheets of printer paper inside for good measure, and the two left the room.

Together, the two officers went back out into the main office, where Brown filled in Derringer on the plan for morning. He would wake up first thing and reserve a ticket on the phone for Elias Derringer to catch the first train out. Rush's wife, Avery, will be bringing breakfast. Once Rush and Derringer had eaten, the deputy would proceed to take him, either by truck or snowmobile, to catch the train in Donneley's Pass headed for Rocky Mount. Brown also reassured the man that the cost of the ticket would be covered by him, and that Derringer shouldn't worry about anything.

With everything organized and planned to a tee, Sheriff Bob Brown left the station with a heavy heart and a knit brow. The guy's pleasant enough, he thought as he climbed into his truck and started it up.

As he rocked the thing back and forth to get it out of the drift that had formed around it, he realized why his chest was so heavy: that guy failed to thank him for the price of the train ticket he would be buying, and he didn't even say goodnight when Bob left the station. He didn't even want to think about the guy's eyes, the way they seemed to look right through you, as if he were reading your thoughts and concentrating real hard. Yes, something was off, all right.

All Sheriff Bob Brown wanted was for the guy to get on that train in the morning and be far away from Thompson Trails as quickly as possible.

CHAPTER 8

"Well, here we are," Rush said in a friendly voice after he had closed and secured the door of the building. He plopped down at his desk and put his feet up immediately. "Hope you got your belly full; if not, I can still heat up that burrito for you."

"I'm good."

Rush began to twiddle his thumbs. Silence was loud, especially if you were in the company of another who was particularly guarded and distant, as this guy was. People like that always made Darren Rush nervous; he was an extrovert to the core, and without conversation, he practically crawled out of his skin. He grabbed up an ancient magazine that Bob kept around for laughs and began to flip through it for the millionth time in his life, but he was soon bored with that as well.

"So, what do you do, Mr. Derringer?" he asked, unable to help himself when it came to not talking.

The stranger sighed and put down the magazine he had been flipping through. "I'm a personal delivery consultant."

Rush got all excited at the fact that the man responded to his question, so he put his feet on the floor and leaned forward. "Really? That sounds cool... better than police work, especially in this Podunk town. So... what does a personal delivery consultant do?" He felt sheepish.

Derringer gave a short chuckle and shook his head at the cop's childlike behavior. "Well, let's see. I, um, consult. With persons. Persons I deliver things to."

Rush nodded and smiled, as if it were as clear as a bell to him, but seconds later, he realized the depth of sarcasm and belittlement the statement really held, and his cheeks flushed red. Darren Rush looked down at his hands, which he had started to twiddle once again, albeit subconsciously.

After a minute, the deputy stood. "I think I'm gonna watch a little television, if you don't mind."

"Actually, I do." Derringer stood up and crossed the cell, stopping at the bars and grasping them with his hands. "I mean, I'm just so exhausted, and I have a pounding headache. I think that's why I was so short with you; sorry about that. Anyway, I'd just really love to get some sleep."

Rush breathed a sigh of relief. The guy wasn't a jerk after all, he just didn't feel good. "No problem, I get it. I'll just dim the lights in here, keep my desk lamp on, and tinker around over here; don't mind me. Oh, and if you need anything, anything at all, don't hesitate to ask."

"Thanks," he replied, backing toward his bunk. "I'm gonna go to sleep now."

The deputy nodded one last time. "Have a good rest, sir."

Elias Derringer didn't answer; he simply turned his back to the man, hiked his wool blanket over his shoulder, and began to doze off.

∞

12:43 a.m.

Elias Derringer snored lightly in his cell, seemingly sleeping like a baby. He had been right, Rush thought. When the guy said he was exhausted, he meant it. There hadn't been so much as a peep from him since the last words they had spoken.

Rush was bored out of his mind and twice as exhausted. So far, the deputy had drunk a full two pots of coffee, and a third was in the process of brewing. Now, he was pacing quietly around the office area just to stay awake. He couldn't play games on his cell phone because the reception was non-existent, and shuffling cards quietly while someone was sleeping could be exhausting. Yes, indeed, coffee was the only thing that could save him now.

As if on cue, the pot stopped churning, and Rush quickly made his way to it, cup in hand. He had just picked up the hot pot and was getting ready to pour when the phone rang. It wasn't a loud ring, really no more than a light series of chirps, but it startled him nonetheless. Who could that be at this time of night? It had to be the sheriff, or else someone was in the middle of a major snowstorm emergency.

Gingerly, Rush put down the pot and cup, then tiptoed to the phone as fast as he could. On his way by, he looked at Derringer; it seemed he hadn't moved a muscle. Not only that, Rush could still hear his faint snoring. The phone hadn't roused him at all.

"Sheriff's Office, Deputy Rush speaking," he answered in a low voice. He knew Sheriff Brown was worried, but calling this late was ridiculous. He'd reassure him right away and get him off the phone.

But it wasn't Sheriff Brown. "Deputy Rush, this is Captain Russell Johnson of the State Patrol. Hope you're having a good night up there in the middle of that snow storm."

"Well, sir, it's pretty bad, but here in Thompson Trails we tend to stay in and wait it out. Makes for strong family ties, if you know what I mean."

The captain chuckled at the joke, then Rush continued. "How can I help you tonight, sir? Hope it isn't anything too bad, considering the hour."

There was a pause on the line. "Well, we can hope not, not for you boys, anyway. Since most of the communication lines are down in a majority of the areas here, we're forced to telephone other law enforcement agencies to make them aware of an active all-points bulletin that is currently in effect. See, we've had a prison convict escape, from Virginia Max, in the last twenty-four hours and a very dangerous one indeed."

Rush hadn't had a call like this since he got his badge. While it was a bit exciting, catching an escapee in Thompson Trails wasn't something he could see happening. He would hear the guy out, document the report, and thank him kindly.

"Who would this be, sir?" he asked.

Johnson cleared his throat. "I'm sure you've heard of Elliot Keller?"

Rush's heart skipped a beat. Of course he'd heard of Elliot Keller. The guy was the sickest of the sick. The things he had done to those girls and that boy in the cabin... Rush shuddered just thinking about it.

"He-he's the one?"

"I'm afraid so. Anyway, we have the APB out, but we are having a hard time getting photos out and about due to lines down." Johnson paused. "If you have a notebook, I can give you a description."

Rush quickly sat at his desk and grabbed a pen. "Shoot."

"White, six-foot-two, approximately one-hundred eighty-five pounds. Long, scraggly black hair, countless tattoos. Keller did have a thick goatee at the time of the escape, but we suspect he shaved it off. Also, two men were killed during the escape, a correctional officer at Virginia Max, and a delivery driver who was dropping off a load of supplies at the prison. Keller made away with the delivery truck; even dressed in the guy's uniform and basically danced right through the gate."

Rush didn't hear most of the last couple of sentences. He was staring into the dimly lit cell not ten feet in front of him. Elias Derringer was still sleeping soundly, light snore and all. His back was to Rush, and it still appeared he was trapped in the throes of his dreams.

"Deputy? Did you hear what I said? He is armed; he has the correctional officer's gun."

Johnson's words snapped him out of it, but he kept his eyes on Derringer and lowered his voice another notch. "I think I might be able to help you with that, Captain."

Another pause, then Johnson replied quietly. "Do you have the inmate, Deputy?"

"Well, I'm not sure, but I believe so."

Rush waited, heart pounding, for Johnson to say something, anything, that wouldn't force an obvious answer from him, an answer that might give away the conversation Rush was having. It wasn't like the guy would be able to do anything if he did hear the conversation; he was in a cell, after all. But the thought of being trapped in the locked jailhouse with a mass murderer while in the middle of a blizzard didn't appeal to the young deputy at all.

"You're not able to talk right now, are you?" Johnson asked.

Rush was relieved. "Not at the current time, but I'm sure that the Sheriff and I will be able to work something out in the future. We often transport prisoners from other counties, but the snow right now makes it virtually impossible. I am sorry to hear about your housing problem, though."

"Okay," Johnson said. "We simply cannot get to you to take him off your hands for obvious reasons. We need you to hold him until the weather lets up and the roads clear; are you able to do that? Is he contained now?"

Rush gave a fake chuckle. "Absolutely. It won't be a problem to continue working it out in just that fashion. That keeps everyone safe. It's never any good to have a conflict in the jail."

"I'm going to get a hold of the Department of Corrections," Johnson continued. "In the morning, I'll call back to discuss the situation with your sheriff, but in the meantime, keep your distance. This man is not to be toyed with, Deputy. Be sure to let your sheriff know immediately. We'll be in touch."

"Will do," Rush replied cheerfully. "Hopefully, we can help you out when the snow clears. You have a good night, now."

Rush hung up the receiver and sat back. Derringer or was it Keller? still hadn't moved. As a matter of fact, it seemed his snoring was a bit deeper. Rush had to think; he had to call the sheriff, and he had to be slick about it.

Quietly, he picked up the receiver and started punching numbers. The sheriff's line rang once, twice, then crackled and went dead. Panicked, Rush hung up to try again, there was no dial tone. Talking to Bob Brown would have to wait until morning.

Only five-and-a-half hours from now…

∞

Keller wasn't sleeping; Keller was wide awake, listening to the one-sided conversation from the cell he was lying in. His fake snoring was effective, as it had always been when incarcerated. But he knew exactly what that call was about, and he knew that there would be no riding with Sheriff Brown to Donneley's Pass, or anywhere else, to catch a train. No, he would be making his way on his own, but before he did that, he had a mess to clean up by the name of Darren Rush.

He could hear Rush trying to dial the phone, and he could hear that the calls weren't going through. What perfect luck! The lines had gone down. Now, he could go ahead and deal with the issue at hand before anyone became wiser to the situation.

Rush would be easy; he was a moron. It took Keller seconds to plan out his escape in his head. Now, all he had to do was wait for the perfect opportunity to go into action.

It wouldn't take long at all with this idiot in charge.

R.W.K. Clark

CHAPTER 9

For the next twenty minutes, Rush sat silently behind the desk, coffee forgotten, staring at Derringer's back as he slept. In his mind, getting the news to the sheriff about their guest could wait until tomorrow, but his stomach was telling him something very different. Rush had a constant nagging feeling that, more than anything, he needed to get Bob Brown on the phone as soon as possible. It wasn't that there was anything they could do about the situation tonight; it was simply the fact that he didn't want to be alone with a guy like this at all, even if there were iron bars between them.

Carefully, the deputy fished his cell phone from the hip pocket of his uniform pants. One look told him that all he had was a single bar; he might just be able to slip a call through to Bob's cell. Checking the land-line one more time, Rush held the receiver to his ear, heard nothing, and replaced it gently in the cradle. Like a mouse, he stood up and crossed the room, then took a left down the small hall to the laundry area; he could pretend to be putting Derringer's clothing in the dryer while he tried Bob again.

Once he had the clothes going, he checked his phone and saw that the bar was gone. Walking around the small room and holding the device in the air proved to do no good at all, so he put it back in his pocket and stopped in his tracks. Darren was starting to panic; he had never dealt with a seriously hardened criminal, and certainly not the likes of this guy. The bottom line was that he was going to be hanging out with this guy until morning, whether he liked it or not, so he might as well accept it. He sure hoped that Bob got there before his wife Avery showed up with breakfast. He didn't want her anywhere near the monster. Darren was half-tempted to hang out in the laundry area until morning; he didn't trust himself not to be taken for a ride, or tricked, by this horrible person who was technically only feet away from him through a wall. No, he couldn't hide; he was a cop! He had to buck up and go out there and do his job.

As he began walking back down the hall toward the front office, he heard the sound. It was a deep, guttural gurgling that sounded about as unearthly as anything he had ever heard. Picking up the pace, Rush sped out front just in time to see Elias Derringer lying on the floor of his cell doing the floppy fish. The seizure appeared to be so bad that the possibility of Derringer swallowing his own tongue was not impossible, and he had foamy drool all around his mouth. Even his eyes were rolled back in his head, his back was arched stiff, and his left leg was kicking here and there at random. At first, Rush just stared at him, his mind racing for answers. But then, all reason left him, and he headed for the cell, keys in hand.

"Oh, no!" Fumbling for the proper key, Rush stood at the door of the cell. "I'm coming, Mr. Derringer; don't you go and die on me now!"

Locating the key, he put it into the lock and turned it, all in one deft movement. Rush dropped to his knees beside the twitching, seizing Derringer and tried to steady the man's head, looking around for something to put into his mouth for him to bite down on.

"It's going to be okay," he said as his eyes scanned the cell. "It's going to be fine."

Suddenly, Elias Derringer's seizure stopped.

Confused, Rush looked down at the man to see him staring up at him and smiling. "Don't you think a night in the hoosegow is much more fun when somebody dies?"

Rush arched an eyebrow, his mind unable to grasp what was happening. One second the guy was seizing; the next, he was talking about good times in the jail.

Cold fear slowly began to creep up Darren Rush's back, making his hair stand on end. In a fraction of a second, he knew he'd been had, and the dread in his stomach was replaced by the acceptance of his own impending death.

Derringer's arm moved, and Rush just caught it out of the corner of his eye. Looking down, he saw that the man had a gun, and it was pointed dead at the center of Rush's chest, the barrel pressing painfully against the skin. His eyes went back to Derringer, and he shook his head helplessly.

"No... please... my wife."

"Don't you worry, Deputy Rush," Keller sneered. "I'll be sure to have plenty of fun with her, too."

The gun went off with a loud bang, and the air instantly began to stink of gunpowder. Blood and bits of flesh were everywhere, including all over Derringer. He kept hold of Rush's dead, but still upright, body, looking him over with intrigue. Keller thought he might never get tired of watching the life drain out of the eyes of another human being. It was one of the most interesting things on Earth to witness. There was no power like it, and he loved it when he was filled with that power. Keller could go without food for weeks if they would just let him kill a couple of people a day.

Finally, he tired of the watching game and let the dead man flop over. He stood and grabbed the deputy's feet, then dragged him to the small mop closet down the hall where the shower and laundry were located, then he covered him with a couple of spare wool blankets. Next, he mopped up the floor, but didn't pay it too much mind. The little missed spots of blood wouldn't matter in the slightest once he was gone, and they wouldn't be noticed right away, should anyone decide to stop in. No one would stop in, though. Not until the dead deputy's wife brought breakfast. Oh, how he was tempted to wait for that little honey. He hadn't had a good piece in a long time.

Keller then began to root through the other closets, and found several police uniforms and hats. He chose a uniform that fit perfectly, then showered and got dressed. Next, he took the deputy's keys and wallet, then left the building, locking it securely behind him.

As soon as he stepped outside, he turned around and smiled. Look! How convenient was this? Deputy dumb butt had parked his truck right in front of the building, as though he wanted to make things as easy on Derringer as possible. It was covered in snow, but that wouldn't be a problem. The white stuff was light and fluffy, and it would take no more than a swish or two of the wipers and a couple of scrapes to clear things up.

As he climbed inside and started the ignition, he thought now was a good time to drop the whole 'Derringer' routine. It was just a temporary ruse, after all. Everyone knew that he was Elliot Keller, and he thought he would keep it that way. Besides, he had sort of come to hate the name Derringer; it was hard enough to answer to some guy's name, and his own was much more fitting to his personality.

Pulling away slowly through the drifting snow, Keller struggled to control the large vehicle. The roads were covered from the snowfall, and the wind had brought drifts the likes of which he had rarely seen. Keller was just getting to the town limits when he caught a patch of ice under the snow and the truck went into a deep skid. The vehicle, which had been going about twenty-five miles-per-hour, slid off the road, down into a ditch, and slammed hard into a massive oak tree.

The airbags deployed, keeping Keller's head from bouncing off the steering wheel, but they did nothing to keep him from being stunned to dizziness. The left side of his head bounced off the driver's side window, forming a gash which gushed plenty of blood and stunned him. He sat there, breathing in and out, trying to get his wits. After about fifteen minutes, he took the

keys from the ignition and got out of the truck. One
look around told him everything he needed to know.
He was in the middle of a pretty bad blizzard, and the
closest place for him to go to keep from freezing to
death was back to the jail. Keller was going to have to
get his head on perfectly straight, figure things out,
and play everything off the best he could when he got
back.

He felt wetness on his temple that was running
down his face, so he reached up and touched the spot.
He looked at his hand, blood. He had managed to
knock himself pretty good in the accident; so much for
the effectiveness of airbags. Keller walked back to the
driver's side door and reached inside to turn the
headlamps off. No need drawing attention before he
even got things figured out. He would leave the truck
right where it was, and by morning, it would be
completely buried. His one regret was that he hadn't
put Rush's body in the truck before leaving. Had he
thought of that, they wouldn't have found the punk
until spring. The thought made him laugh.

He began to stagger off, back in the direction of
the jail. He stayed off the main road mostly, walking to
the side in the deep drifts. He was freezing cold, but
his mind was on too many other things to let that get
to him. Keller was busy thinking about the gun he still
had in his pocket, the one he had escaped from

Virginia Max with. The fact that they hadn't frisked him and found it had been nothing short of a miracle, though Keller adamantly refused to believe in miracles. In order to have a miracle happen, there had to be a god, and there was no such being in Keller's reality whatsoever. Anyway, he still had the gun, and it still had some bullets in it, so no matter what happened after he returned, he would have his own back easily enough. Besides, when he returned to the jail, he could take Rush's weapon, plus any others he could get his hands on, along with ammo. He would be set up but good.

With the high drifts and winds, it took Keller more than forty-five minutes to get back to the jail. He didn't see one car, nor light from any of the residences he passed. The town was dead, which calmed him. Soon enough, he'd be back in that warm bunk in a clean pair of scrubs, and whoever happened to pop in next would be none the wiser to anything that had gone on between him and Deputy Rush, and they would be oblivious to the call that Rush had gotten from the State Patrol.

At last, he reached the sheriff's office. He fumbled with the keys briefly, then let himself back inside, locking it behind him once again. Turning up the lights a bit, he noticed a couple of blood spots he had missed on the floor, so the first thing he did was grab the mop and get that cleaned up. Next, he went to the back and changed out of the cop uniform and into a fresh pair of prisoner scrubs from the same closet where the uniforms were kept, making sure to tuck Deputy Rush's wallet into his underwear. Bagging up the uniform and bloody mop head, he went out the back door and threw them into the dumpster, then went back inside to warm up once again. He also took the deputy's gun, found some ammo in the guy's desk, and took it all into the cell.

Dimming the lights, Keller took Rush's keys and locked himself back inside the cell, then hid the keys and gun under the fire-retardant plastic mattress he would be sleeping on. He tucked himself in and let out a long, tired sigh. It wasn't going to take him long to fall asleep. Not even the mystery of who he would have to deal with next was enough to keep him awake. In his mind, the one thing he had to worry about was the arrival of the State Patrol, and he had time to figure out a plan before they made their way to him to take him back. No, now was the time to get some sleep.

The last conscious thought Elliot Keller had consisted of wishing that he had heard the entirety of the phone conversation between Rush and the State Patrol. That would have enabled him to plan much more quickly and efficiently. He knew they were going to be coming, but it certainly wouldn't be tonight. No one in this part of the state was going anywhere tonight, but they would arrive to fetch him soon enough.

But for now, it was time to get some sleep, because he was most definitely going to need it.

∞

Keller had a dream.

He was in the basement, the wet, moldy, stinky basement, with his wet, stinky blanket. There was a rat in the corner, and it would taunt him with its squealing. Sometimes, it would come out and nip at his little boy toes, but when he screamed, it would run back into the shadows.

The basement room was different this time; it didn't have a rotting wooden door, like it always had. Instead, it had bars. He looked down at his body, and in the slivers of light that came through the bars he could see he was wearing striped jail clothes, like on TV. He thought they looked clean, which was strange; his parents never gave him clean clothes for as long as he could remember.

"Hey, boy! Are you feeling a bit hungry? Or are you just bored?"

His father's voice brought panic, and he chose not to answer. If he answered, it was always wrong, so little Elliot had learned to keep his mouth shut. But right now, he could tell that his father wasn't alone. He was dragging someone down the stairs with him, and that person was struggling.

Suddenly, the lights came on, blinding him and causing him to cover his face. When he opened his eyes, he saw his father standing there with a smile on his face. He was holding his mother, who was bound with rope, tightly by the arm. She had duct tape over her mouth, and she was crying heavily. In the other hand, his father held what appeared to be a single cookie. They had been his favorite, and his mouth began to water.

His father threw his mother hard to the dirt floor, and her head bounced off it. She lay there, limp and crying, as her husband unlocked the cell door. He waved the cookie at his son.

"Do you want the cookie, Elliot? If you do, you have to let me do one thing."

Elliot nodded eagerly, his stomach screaming for the tiny bit of food.

The man set the cookie on one of the crossbars of the cell door. "Now, don't you try to grab it! You just lay there and let me do what I gotta do, and when I'm done, you can eat that cookie, okay, Elliot?"

He nodded again.

His father reached into his pocket and pulled out two small safety pins, then he approached the small child. He laid him on the wet mattress and straddled him, pinning his arms beneath his knees.

"Now, Elliot, this will hurt for a second, but it will feel good for a lifetime."

His father, his daddy, began to put the pins through his eyelids and forehead skin, pinning his eyes open so he couldn't blink or close them without horrific pain. He sat the boy up and propped him against the rotten concrete wall.

"Now, you watch how I teach your mother a lesson, and you can have your cookie."

For the next hour, Elliot Keller watched his father do the most unspeakable things to his mother that could be imagined. Not only did it tear his heart and mind apart, but gave him chills that he didn't understand. When it was over, his father kicked his mother around a bit until she was unconscious. Next, he quickly removed the safety pins, then took the cookie from the bar and looked at his bleeding son.

"Did you like that?"

Elliot nodded, his mouth watering for the cookie.

"Good. Because I like cookies."

The man popped the entire cookie into his own mouth, locked the cell, grabbed Elliot's mother, and went back upstairs. Elliot cried until he was no longer conscious...

∞

Elliot woke, furious and shaking. It might have been a dream, but it was based on a reality that had happened to him over and over and over, until Elliot Keller had finally killed both of his parents and buried them under the dirt in the basement at the age of fifteen. He became a ward of the state, because they considered him a deserted youth.

Yes, all of that had been bad and painful at the time. His father had made him the man he was today.

R.W.K. Clark

CHAPTER 10

By five o'clock the next morning, the snow in Thompson Trails was showing absolutely no signs of letting up. As a matter of fact, it was falling like mad, almost as if there were an avalanche coming straight down from heaven. The entire town was on emergency status, and it was made clear over the radio that no one was to venture out in their vehicles to try and brave the roads for any reason. If any traveling must be done, it was to be done using snowmobiles. Fortunately, the townsfolk all had one, but most of them wouldn't be using them that day.

Avery Rush stood in the kitchen of the small, cozy home she shared with her husband, Darren. She was packing an insulated cooler with plates of hot breakfast food wrapped in foil: eggs, bacon, pancakes, and hashed browns. She also had two clean water bottles filled with cold milk, as well as silverware and napkins inside. She zipped the cooler shut and walked over to the window to get a look outside. Shaking her head, she put on her heavy parka, and thought how miserable the snowmobile ride to the station was going to be. Fortunately for her, she had started the contraption ten minutes ago, so it would be raring to go by the time she was ready to head out.

Avery wrapped her scarf tightly around her face and neck, then donned a thick woolen cap before pulling her parka hood over it all. Next, she put on her insulated gloves, grabbed the cooler, and headed out the door, neglecting to lock it behind her. After all, no one in Thompson Trails ever really locked their doors, unless they were banks or other such businesses. Either way, she didn't think twice about it; she just hopped on the snowmobile after securing the cooler with bungee cords and aimed the vehicle through the snow drifts towards the sheriff's office.

Her thoughts on the way were light and carefree. Sure, the snow was overwhelming, but man, was it beautiful. Even as it fell, it rested on the branches of the trees like lace, giving the entire town a clear look of perfection, almost postcard-worthy. She smiled beneath her scarf, and considered how happy she had been since she had married Darren Rush. Everything was working out for her according to plan.

Avery hadn't told him yet; she had been saving it for his birthday, which was right around the corner. It's a boy; she was simply beside herself with joy. Even though Darren was a man, and he absolutely withheld any feelings he had that were less than 'manly,' she knew he would be just as excited as she was. Even now, as she rode that stupid snowmobile around the corner to the sheriff's office, she could swear that she could feel the tiny life growing inside of her, which was impossible, of course. After all, she was just over two months along.

The first thing Avery noticed as she neared the station was the fact that Darren's truck was gone. At first, it was enough to make her crinkle her nose in confusion; wasn't he supposed to be staying all night because of the drifter? After less than a moment's thought, she pushed her concern from her mind. For all she knew, perhaps Bob Brown had to borrow Darren's truck. It was Thompson Trails, after all; nothing should surprise her when it came to the simple workings of this small town.

Avery slowed the snowmobile and pulled it next to the space that should have been occupied by her husband's truck. It seemed that there was much less snow drifting in that spot, and she figured that either Darren or Bob, whoever had the vehicle, would be able to maneuver into that spot much easier when they returned. For now, she needed to get the food inside.

She left the vehicle running and released the cooler from the bungee wraps. Stopping long enough to fish the station keys from her parka pocket, she was soon heading up to the door and letting herself in. The lighting inside was still dim, the way they kept it when they had inmates. Not only that, but the typically musty-smelling station was exuding the stale smell of pennies, something Avery had never caught in the air which filled the building. She stopped dead and looked around the dimly lit room before reaching to her right and adjusting the tone of the lighting. The room was empty, and it smelled of bleach and pennies. After a moment, her eyes focused enough to see that the 'guest' was sleeping soundly, locked in the cell, with his back to her. She could even hear his light snoring.

"Ex-excuse me," she uttered timidly. "Hello, sir?"

The man squirmed and moaned, then seemed to settle right back into his sleep. Avery's eyes were scanning the station like mad; where was Darren? Where was Sheriff Bob?

"Darren? Honey? I'm here with breakfast." He was likely in the restroom. Regardless of the weird aroma and the fact that he wasn't present, she knew her husband, and he was definitely in the restroom first thing in the morning.

Her words managed to rouse the man in the cell, however. He suddenly turned over and made immediate contact with her. A smile grew quickly over his face, and his black eyes seemed to pierce her own cornflower blue ones. Avery shivered and fought the temptation to holler for her husband one more time.

"Well, hello pretty lady," the man said as he swung his feet to the floor. "You must be the deputy's missus."

Avery smiled shyly, but her eyes continued to rapidly scan the room, and her ears refused to stop listening for any sound that signified she was not alone with this stranger.

"Yes, I am," she replied in a soft tone. "I brought breakfast for you two men. Where's Deputy Rush?"

The man gave a chuckle, stood, and gave a long, leisurely stretch, as though he had just woken up, but he had been wide awake for hours. "I'm not sure. I think something happened with Sheriff Bob's snowmobile, and he went to help the man put it in order. He said he would be back shortly; he's been gone about a half-hour. How're the streets out there, anyway? Any sign of things clearing up?"

Avery relaxed a bit and placed the cooler on Darren's desk, where she proceeded to open it and get the breakfast items ready. "No, not really. As a matter of fact, they expect the storm to last at least two more days, and the plows won't even be able to hit the roads to clear until after that. This is the worst storm since I was a kid, I gotta tell ya." Avery gave a nervous laugh.

Keller listened politely, entertained by her edgy nervousness. As he watched her trembling hands and anxious disposition, he was amused. It tickled him that his presence set her on edge. That was the exact sort of thing that turned him on the most.

Avery took up his plate, bottle of milk, and silverware wrapped in a napkin, and made her way to his cell. "I'm not exactly sure how to get this in there to you," she said with a smile. "Usually, one of the men is here to take care of that."

Keller took two short steps to the cell door, grabbed a couple of the bars, and smiled out at her alluringly. "No worries, pretty lady. Deputy Rush left the keys to the cell with me. He said you might be here before he gets back." Keller dangled them outward in her direction. "See? Here they are."

Avery stared at him, her smile fake, and her nerves alarmingly real. "Um... would you please unlock the door? There isn't any way for me to get this in to you unless you do."

The man continued to look at her with his eerie smile, dangling the keys continually, as if he were trying to hypnotize her with them. Why did he look so familiar to her? There was something about him, something inside of her that was trying to tell her that she had seen him somewhere before, and it hadn't been a good thing, whatever it was.

Keller chose a key on the ring. He paused right before reaching through the bars to put the key in the hole, looking up at her once again. "So, have you talked to Sheriff Brown? I assume he'll be heading down here soon? I'm ready to get on the road to Rocky Mount, and he's supposed to be buying me a ticket and sending me on my way."

"I haven't spoken to him, but if he said that's what he was going to do, you can count on it happening."

She turned to offer him a nervous smile, but there was never a chance to fully give him one. Before she could even take a breath or be surprised, Keller grabbed Avery in a bear hug, squeezing her so tightly she could neither breathe nor scream. She began to kick her legs frantically, her heels coming into hard contact with his knees and shins, but the blows didn't faze Keller at all. The twisted man simply began to laugh, amused by the entire confrontation.

Suddenly, he flung her to the floor, where Avery began to cough and scramble to get away from him. He watched her for a brief moment, entertained, then chased her, grabbed her by the ankles, and dragged her backward until they were by the Deputy's desk.

"I say we have a little fun before we eat our breakfast," he offered. "Might as well take advantage of all of this alone time."

"Please, don't," she sobbed. "I'm pregnant!"

Keller laughed hard. "Oh, goody! Two little birds with one giant stone!"

Keller lifted her up and flung her down on top of the Deputy's desk hard, knocking the wind from her lungs. As she lay there struggling to breathe, Keller began to tear at her snowsuit, throwing each piece here and there as it was shed. Finally, after all the struggling, he was able to remove her jeans. He put his hands down hard on her shoulders and leaned over into her face, looking her in the eyes and smiling.

"Now for a little fun," he sneered.

Suddenly, Avery's arm swung forward and around. Keller felt a sharp sting down the length of his right arm, and a surprised look came over his face; she had a letter opener in her hand, and his blood was dripping from it and running down her wrist.

"Oh, you want to play?"

Keller grabbed her by the shoulders and shook her hard, like a rag doll. Her head slammed off the desk, stunning her, and that was when he grabbed her by her head, twisted one time, hard, and snapped her neck instantly. Avery was gone, and the child inside of her struggled itself to death.

Keller stopped and put his hand to his arm, then looked at his own blood on his hand. You little… he thought. Oh, well. Either way, she was going to die that day; there was nothing she could have done to save her own life. With a smile, Keller proceeded to have his way with her dead body, right there on the Deputy's desk. When he was finished, he went to the station door and locked it.

He went back to the restroom area and looked in the mirror at his bloody arm. The wound was long and gaping, and the very sight of it made him smile. She'd done a good job for having nothing other than a letter opener for a weapon. He thought about finding a sewing kit and trying to stitch it up, but he had two reasons not to: the sheriff would be there soon, for one, and secondly, he liked the way it looked. It added to his natural good looks.

Leaving the bathroom, Keller took a look outside the window. The woman's snowmobile was there, still running, but he didn't want to risk taking it when the sheriff was due any minute. No, he was going to tuck himself away with his gun behind the station door, and there he was going to patiently wait for Johnny Law to come in and find the mess he had made. Then, and only then, would Keller wrap up the little party he had at the Sheriff's Office. After that, he had other business to attend to in Thompson Trails: unfinished business.

With gun and letter opener in hand, Keller took his place behind the station door, hiding himself behind a rack of coats that had been standing there, dusty, who knew how long. He was well hidden, and he knew it. Now there was nothing for him to do but wait, and Keller was very patient.

CHAPTER 11

The snow continued to dump from the sky. Everything was white, even the sky above, and the sun, though obviously out, could not be seen at all. Sheriff Bob Brown stood next to his snowplow in his driveway, staring upward and praying that the weather would soon enough take a turn for the better.

He climbed inside of the cab of his truck and lowered the plow. Rose stood inside at the large picture window, smiling and waving at him. She blew him a kiss, and he reciprocated happily. She was so beautiful, his Rosie. It always made his heart ache to leave her in the morning, and the only thing that kept him going throughout the day was the firm knowledge that she was home, waiting for him, baking a pie and keeping his supper warm with her love.

Bob pulled out of the driveway and took a right, plowing the piles of snow on the streets as he went. It would take him a bit of extra time to get to the station today because of this. He knew that Darren was likely exhausted, but there was always that cot that was tucked along the wall in the short hallway; if he had to, he could just take a quick nap, or even get a couple of good hours' sleep in. Suddenly, Bob's stomach lurched violently, and it confused him. What was that about? It wasn't nausea, but more like nervousness or dread. He sure hoped everything was okay down there. He had tried to call Darren before he left, but the lines were still down. He would just have to find out what was going on when he got there.

For the next half-hour, Bob plowed the main strip through town, on his way to the station, but it was being covered again just as fast as he was clearing it. He would wait until things cleared up, then he would come back out and get back to work on the street. But that wouldn't be until they got rid of Derringer so he could catch the train at Donneley's Pass. Overall, the sheriff felt good, but when he thought about getting rid of that weirdo Derringer, he felt even better.

He was just about fifty yards away when he noticed how off things were at the station. Darren's vehicle was gone, and it appeared that Avery's snowmobile was practically buried in the snow, and it appeared to be still running. How long had she been there? Where was Darren's truck? All at once, something inside of the sheriff fell ill, and he knew without having to guess that all dismay had broken loose at the Sheriff's Office. He was scared to death to go inside and look.

Bob pulled up to the station, concern on his face as he looked the building over. Everything appeared to be quiet, with the exception of the idling sound from the snowmobile. No one came to the window to see who was pulling up, and that was more than odd, in his opinion. His stomach gave another lurch; something was wrong... very wrong. If it was, indeed, it was he who had done wrong. Somewhere along the line, he had let his heart do his thinking for him. He had been fooled, and he knew it before he even got out of the truck.

Leaving the old truck running, Bob jumped out of the cab and headed for the station. He jiggled the knob, but it was locked tight. Giving the door a couple of hard thumps, he shouted a couple times, but he got nothing but silence in return. He knit his brow and fished his keys out of his pocket with trembling hands. He felt sick to his stomach; there was some kind of smell he was picking up, something that seemed to be wafting from under the door.

"Darren, open the door, would you?" he shouted as he slipped the key into the hole. "It's colder than an icebox out here! Avery? Darren?"

Bob turned the key and the lock slid into the open position. He turned the knob and opened the door, noticing right away that the lights were set to just above the dim position that was used at night when they had inmates. The lights should have been set on high by now. Stepping inside, Bob closed the door and reached for the switch and turned the lights all the way up.

"Oh, no!"

The first thing his eyes fell on was Avery Rush. She was on her back on top of Darren's desk, naked from the waist down and her legs splayed open grotesquely. Blood had gushed from between them, along with some sort of tissue, and it was running down the side of the desk. Bob immediately doubled over and vomited on the floor right in front of him. He continued to do so until he could do nothing but dry heave, then he wiped his mouth, covered his mouth and nose with his hand, and made his way to her.

"Oh, Avery! Darren! Darren, where are you?"

Bob looked at the cell to see that the door was wide open; Elias Derringer was not inside, nor was he anywhere in the main office. Drawing his gun, Bob began to slowly walk toward the short hall, holding his breath to keep from puking, and purposefully averting his eyes from the pretty dead woman on his desk. He took a left down the hall to find nothing in view, then began to open each and every door one at a time. It wasn't until he opened the small mop closet in the back that he found the body of his deputy, a massive hole blown through his chest. His eyes were still open. Whatever had taken place here, whoever that stranger really was, Sheriff Bob Brown knew with great certainty that he was neither equipped nor experienced enough to deal with the likes of this guy.

"Oh, Darren," he muttered, the back of his hand against his mouth. "What happened here?"

Sheriff Brown began to back out of the closet and up the hall, his hand still covering his mouth to keep the vomit from coming up. He was in shock, and though his gun was in his hand, he was no longer aware of its presence. It shook loosely in his hand like a doll getting ready to fall from the hands of a crying little girl.

At the end of the hall, by the doorway to the main station office, he bumped hard into the wall, which proved to bring him back to reality. He had to think; he had to contact someone, do something! But the phones were out, and so was the Internet, and he was in a world of trouble. It was all he could do to hope that the guy had stolen Darren's truck and had gotten out of Dodge.

He had to find a way to get some help to Thompson Trails before anything worse happened here. Holstering his weapon, he was sure that Elias Derringer had taken Darren's truck now, and there was no telling where the guy was at this point. How had someone with such a clean record been able to do something so vile, so horrendous?

Bob turned into the office area and stopped dead in his tracks. There stood Derringer, a gaping, bloody wound running down his arm, and a smile on his face. His soulless eyes were smiling too, and he looked to Bob like a kid who had been waiting a very long time for a party that was just getting ready to begin.

"Well, hello, Sheriff Brown," he said with a broad grin. "I'm sure you're surprised at all the gifts I've left for you. I did all of this out of thanks, you know. For your small-town hospitality and all of that." He paused and glanced at Avery. "She was special, and so was the child she was carrying; I left her in return for the cold, crusty donut. Thanks a lot, you pig."

Bob yearned for the safety of his gun, the man looked to him with evil and anger in his eyes. He shook the gun he was holding at Bob and sneered.

"The first thing you are going to do is undo your utility belt, put it on the floor and kick it over here to me, now!"

Keeping his eyes on the stranger, Bob did as he was told. He felt anger mingle in with the sickness he felt in his belly. "What have you done, Derringer? What in the heck is wrong with you?"

The murderer laughed loudly, throwing his head back as he did so. A shiver of terror ran down Bob's spine. He had a terrible feeling he wasn't going to be walking out of the Sheriff's Office alive that day.

"What have I done, you ask?" The man began to pace, and as he did, Bob noticed that the guy was holding his silver letter opener in the other hand. He waved them around as he walked and thought about what his answer was going to be. "First, we should probably get on a first name basis. I'll call you 'Bob,' just Bob. I think that's a fitting name for you, you fat tub of lard."

"Now, back to the first name thing," the man said as he picked up Bob's gun and tucked it into the waistband of his scrub pants. "As you may or may not know by now, I am not 'Elias Derringer.' My name is Elliot Keller; pleased to make your acquaintance."

Elliot Keller? Bob's stomach sank to the floor and dropped like lead into the soles of his feet. Oh, this man was a mass murderer, one of the sickest dirtballs in existence. But he was in prison, serving time for all his crimes, wasn't he? Obviously not.

"None of this would have happened if it hadn't been for a call your deputy received last night from The State Patrol." Keller leaned on Darren's desk and clucked his tongue. "They told him I had escaped, and to be on the lookout. Deputy Rush knew he had me, and he tried to call you, but needless to say, the phones happened to go out right after he hung up. Poor Darren; I really didn't have any other choice, not that it bothered me to put a big pit in his chest. He was such a Barney Fife... how could you even consider having a sidekick like that? Look at the results of his stupidity!"

"What about poor Avery?" Bob asked. "Why Avery?"

"Why Avery?" Keller's voice was mocking and nasty, and he gave nothing more than a casual shrug. "Cuz I needed some lovin', that's why. It's really nothing more than that. She had some pretty good cooze for a dead chick. I have to admit, though, the best part was knowing that the baby inside of her was slowly dying. My youngest victim yet."

Bob gagged, and then vomit shot out of his mouth again. As he puked, Keller laughed. When Bob was finished, he looked up at the convict, mad he had dropped his gun to the floor, and now he was as defenseless as all of them had been against this mass murderer. "My turn, huh? The least you could do is give me a head start." Bob begged.

Keller nodded. "Yes sir, it is your turn, but there will be no head starts."

With that, Keller fired three consecutive shots at Sheriff Brown. The first two hit him in the chest, making him dance like a drunk marionette. The third took out part of his skull and brain, and he dropped to the floor with a heavy thud.

He walked over to the sheriff and dug through his pockets until he had his wallet, badge, and a large ring of keys. Next, he went to the front window and took note that the sheriff had come in the pickup with the plow attached. It was perfect, still running and warm. Time to get out of here, but before he left Thompson Trails for good, he intended to have a bit more fun.

Keller definitely hadn't forgotten about sweet Donna Welk, or her vile husband. The fun he could have with them would compare greatly to his own upbringing, but they wouldn't survive it like he had. He shouldn't have, wished he hadn't, but he had, and now there was a penalty to pay for everyone he came into contact with.

Keller struggled to take Brown's parka off, making sure there were gloves in the pockets. Not only did he find gloves, but he also found a nice warm hunting hat as well. He was in a bit of a hurry, so he put the coat on, mindless of the big holes in the front from the bullet wounds. Keller put on the hat, then the gloves, then loaded the pockets with the wallets of his victims. Time to get out of Dodge.

He stepped out into the icy day and locked the jail behind him. Putting his face toward the sun, Keller took a deep breath of fresh air and smiled. When he opened his eyes, a snowmobile was just passing; it was the blond woman Donna, from the cabin resort. Yummy, he thought to himself, just the person he intended to pay a visit to. Things couldn't be more perfect. He stood still, smiled at her, and waved. Man, oh man, was luck on his side the last couple of days, or what?

Donna Welk waved back and pulled the snowmobile over to the side of the road. She left the vehicle running, then climbed off and trudged her way to Keller through the drifts, still smiling pleasantly. This was going to be much easier than he thought; he grinned back in a friendly manner, then reached out and opened the passenger side door of the running pickup.

"I see you're still here in our little burg," she said with a sniffle. "Going somewhere with Sheriff Brown? Did he manage to get you a train ticket?"

Keller nodded and tossed the thermal gloves he had been wearing on the passenger seat. "Yeah, he's running me to Donneley's Pass to catch the train to Rocky Mount. Sure is a friendly guy; he let me sleep here, fed me, and even bought my train ticket for me; wouldn't even hear of me paying him back. Couldn't ask for a better sheriff."

Donna nodded. "We like him. So, you're from Rocky Mount, or are you just visiting family there?"

"Just visiting."

Keller paused in the door and pretended to fiddle around with something on the front seat, just out of Donna's sight. She was looking skyward, squinting at the white that seemed to be all around them. She then looked back at him and shivered.

"Yes, he'd do just about any–" Suddenly, she stopped.

Keller looked back at her to see that her smile was gone; she was staring at the front of the parka he was wearing. He knew exactly what she was looking at, but he looked down as well, just for good measure.

"What happened to you? Is that blood? Mr. Derringer, there's a huge hole! Are you okay?"

Donna no sooner got the words out of her mouth than Keller grabbed a huge Maglite that was sitting in the middle of the bench-style seat in the truck. He gave a glance up and down the street and turned back to her, keeping the Maglite out of sight just behind the door.

"Yeah, I guess it is," he replied with a chuckle. "It's pretty much a bloody mess in there, too. You ought to see what I did to those people." Keller nodded toward the station house and laughed cheerfully. Then he looked back at Donna, smile gone, and said, "But not as much of a mess as it's going to be for you in a minute."

"Wha-?"

With a single hard swing, Keller brought the Maglite up into the air, then brought it down on her head so hard that a stream of blood shot out of the gash it created. Donna Welk crumpled to the ground with nothing more than a squeak, and she lay there in the snow while the blood seeped from her head, turning white to red.

Keller tossed the light back into the truck and looked up and down the street one more time. Not a person in sight, and not a single human sound came from any direction. He picked her up from the ground as though she weighed no more than a bag of feathers, and Keller put her in the passenger side of the pickup, laying her over toward the middle. Locking the passenger door, he pulled the parka hood up, went around the plow in the front, and climbed into the driver's side. Soon, he was pulling away from the station, leaving nothing but murder and blood behind them.

Elliot Keller wasn't sure where he was going, but he figured he had plenty of time to figure it out in a town as dead as Thompson Trails was right at that moment in time. The best thing he could think of to do was take the truck down the main road, by where he had wrecked. He could pull down by the icy water and sit there and think about his next move. Even if she woke while they were there, she would have no hope for escape.

They would literally be in the middle of nowhere.

R.W.K. Clark

CHAPTER 12

Keller found it easier to maneuver the roads of Thompson Trails with Sheriff Bob's pickup and the attached plow. The snow was still falling in what could be called torrents, but he had the plow down, and the snow was moving out of his way like countless scared rabbits recognizing a great big gun coming at them. It was calming, and the serenity of the control motivated him to turn on the radio. An old country song pumped through the tinny speakers initially, but Keller fixed that by tracking down a station that was playing a slamming song by a heavy metal group, and it turned his good mood into one that was great.

As he drove, he thought about the bleeding Donna Welk passed out next to him in the passenger seat. He could hear rattled breathing coming from her lungs, and the blood on her head was clotting quite nicely. Elliot Keller felt no amount of remorse or pity for the blond woman, even though she had been kind and trusting toward him. Instead, it seemed he could smell her womanhood coming off of her in great waves, and his mind seemed to be wrapped around what he would do to her when he had the chance. He wouldn't be pursuing these actions while they were parked near the river; no, he would wait until he could take her to that prick of a husband of hers. That was when he would have the most fun. That was when he would be sure to put her through every level of purgatory he could fathom, and he would do it before the eyes of the man who had promised to care for her and protect her every day of the rest of her life. The thought of doing these things thrilled him to the bone. Even when he was captured, he would thrive on the memory of her pain for the remainder of his days. Oh, yes, he would make sure that he had more fun with Donna Welk than he had with any of the 'lovers' he had taken before her, even if she was the last he ever got his hands on.

Suddenly, she began to stir. At first, she gave nothing but slight moans and whimpers. Then she started to move a bit, squirming and jerking here and there, as if she were trying to come to life and get her wits about her. He glanced over at her and laughed, then reached out and turned down the radio. Shifting his eyes between the road and Donna, he kept his amused smile on his face and waited for the woman to come to enough to have some kind of conversation with.

"Wha -? What's going...?"

Keller snickered, pleased with her confused and frightened tone. "Well hello, Mrs. Welk! It's about time you decided to join the party! I was wondering if you were going to cop out on me or continue to be the life of the party since I met you. The sweet little blondie that I first laid eyes on. You know, Donna, I can smell you from here, and you smell as sweet as a school girl, if you know what I mean."

Donna lifted herself up on one elbow, groaned, and grabbed at her head with one hand. "It hurts," she muttered. "What's happening... where am I?"

Now, Keller laughed in earnest. "Where are you? Don't you know? You mean to tell me that you don't remember me? You don't remember our little meeting a couple of days ago? The way your lousy husband called the cops on me when all I was trying to do was keep warm?"

Now she lifted herself up a bit more, grabbing the door handle with her hand for support. Shifting in her seat, she touched her head once again, this time looking at the semi-dried tacky blood that was smeared over the palm of her hand. She turned to him, and even though her eyes were distant and dizzy, she seemed to be recollecting what was really going on.

143

"Mr. Derringer?" she asked, unsure.

Keller snickered. "Yeah, I guess so. At least, as far as you know. But you might know me better as Elliot Keller. Do you know me, Donna Welk? Elliot Keller?"

She observed him for a moment, and much to his surprise, the woman remained more than calm. "Yes, I know about you Mr. Keller."

Elliot glanced at her, his smile fading a bit. Why was she so calm? "You know about me, do you? What do you know about me, Donna Welk?"

She clenched her eyes shut against the pain of her pounding head. "I know you. I know what you do, and I know who you are."

"Tell me."

Donna leaned her aching head against the cold glass of the passenger side window. "You like to hurt women. You would like to hurt me."

"Let me tell you something, Donna Welk," he muttered with an entertained grin. "You don't know what being hurt is all about. All you know about me you've heard on television or read in the papers. I want you to know that they just give half the story, the tame parts. Honey, I'm going to do things to you that you never imagined possible."

Keller took his eyes off the road long enough to really study her. She seemed completely unafraid, as if she had resigned herself to the fact of what he had planned in the few short minutes since she had gained consciousness. He was impressed, to say the least. She wasn't even looking toward the door, like she was thinking of jumping. It wouldn't have helped; she wouldn't be going anywhere without him.

"Yes, I would like to hurt you," he replied. "But more than that, I am going to hurt you. As soon as the time is right, I am going to show you pain like you have never known. But none of that is going to take place without Mr. Rick, your dear husband. He needs to witness all of it."

They were well past the place where Keller had wrecked Rush's truck, and now he saw that there was a turn off up ahead that led down to a small parking area by the river. The road they were on was flanked by the river on both sides, with multiple small drive-downs that allowed tourists or other visitors to park. The one up ahead was perfect, so it seemed. It not only left the road and allowed them to be out of view of passing cars, but it also gave them room to park under a large tree. Keller slowed down the truck and put on the blinker, even though there was not another car in sight to warn of his intentions.

For all of her dizziness, Donna took notice of his intentions clearly. "Whatever you do, be careful going down there. The water toward the river's edge is going to give way if you're not careful; we'll both go under and drown, and you won't be having much fun with me then, will you, Mr. Keller?"

Her condescending attitude pissed him off, but at the same time it gained a bit of his respect. Donna Welk didn't seem to have any kind of fear of him. She seemed to just be in clear acceptance of his intent, and in a way, that scared him. All of his victims buckled and begged. They cried for their lives and the lives of their friends and loved ones. But not Donna Welk; if anything, the only thing she conveyed was calm disgust, and it unnerved him a bit. If he had met her in another life, he just might have fallen in love with her.

"I think I can handle it without any help from you, Donna."

She snorted at him. "I've lived here a bit longer than you've been around. And don't call me Donna."

Keller swung out with his right arm and smashed her in the face, causing blood to spurt full-force from her nose. She cried out, slightly, and put the sleeve of her parka to her face. Then she started to laugh at him. What a weakling, to hit a woman. What a coward!

"If you're going to kill me anyway, what do I care what your opinion is?" She laughed some more, then wiped at her nose, blood smearing across her cheek. "By the time you're done with me, this little bit of blood will be nothing." She turned to him and sneered. "You're nothing but a lowlife, and you can't threaten me enough to scare me. Let's just get on with business, jerk."

Keller didn't answer, but he was furious with her blasé attitude. He took a slow right down into the turn-off and pulled up under the tree, aiming the nose of the heavy truck at the edge of the river. It was hard to tell how close he was to the water because the snow was so deep and drifting, but he didn't care; surely the ice was thick enough to hold them. Besides, he didn't give much credence to anything one of his victims said to him; they were blabbering in futile efforts to save their lives.

"So," he said sarcastically as he slowly steered the pickup and plow down into the pull-off. "I can't threaten you enough to scare you, huh? You seem awfully sure of yourself, and I find that amusing. You have no idea what I'm capable of, so keep that in mind."

"You have no idea what I know or don't know, so you keep that in mind, you coward." Donna spat.

Donna Welk knew exactly what this monster was capable of, and she knew one thing and one thing only: she had never known a pain like that she felt regarding the loss of a child, or the hope of having one. It made her want to die. He could do what he wanted to do; death would take her into the presence of the child she never held. Most of all, she was worried about Rick, not herself.

"Keller, you're pulling a bit too close to the water's edge," she said wearily. "I'm trying to tell you –"

"Shut up! The water's so frozen that it would probably hold us safely until spring, you dumb cooze." Keller insisted.

Donna rolled her eyes and shrugged, then put her fingers back to the wound on her head. It was terribly sore, but it seemed that the blood was clotting quite nicely, and surprisingly enough, her head and thinking were incredibly clear for the blow he had dealt her. She kept her mouth shut as Keller crept closer and closer to the snow drift which hid the ice at the water's edge.

"I'm telling you, Keller…"

Suddenly, there was a loud crack. It sounded more like a very loud gunshot, and as soon as it occurred, the front end of the truck, heavy from the extra weight of the plow attachment, sank about a half-foot with a violent jerk. Keller's eyes flew open in surprise, and Donna rolled her own once again.

"I told you, you stupid dirtbag."

"Shut up!" Keller hit her again, causing nothing more than a groan, and the front end of the truck jerked again, sinking a bit more. He paused and listened, as if trying to determine if they were going to sink any more than they already had. Sure enough, another pop, then a large crevice began to form and creep across the river at an alarming rate of speed. Keller grabbed her violently by the shoulder of her parka and jerked her across the bench seat, opening the driver's door at the same time. "We have to get out of here, and now!"

For the first time, Donna Welk didn't disagree with him. Slight vertigo aside, she allowed him to pull her, and she scrambled to follow him. Neither of them had any idea how far out he had actually pulled into the river, but she knew that it was far enough that the heavy truck was going to sink, at least the front end. They couldn't stay in the truck and expect to survive.

The truck jerked downward once again, this time sinking another foot-and-a-half. Donna saw the panic come over Keller's face as they both fell from the driver's side and landed hard in the snow drift running alongside the truck. As they sat in the freezing snow, breathing hard, both of them watched the entire front end of the truck submerge, and it didn't take long for the rest of the vehicle to follow suit. In no time at all, it was out of sight, nothing but bubbles rising to the surface as it sank to the bottom of the river and completely out of sight.

The pair sat in silence, staring at the empty spot that now consisted of nothing but tire tracks and plow skid marks. Donna wanted to laugh out loud, but it wouldn't be worth it to piss off the startled murderer any more than he already was. At last, she giggled a bit, stopped herself, and then just waited patiently for him to tell her what to do next. It didn't take long to find out.

Keller grabbed her once again by the parka and jerked her to her feet, joining her as they went. "Looks like we're running out of obvious options, but I'm not done with you yet. How far are we from your cabins?"

She ignored the question. "What do you want me to do?" she asked. "Lay down naked right here and let you do your vile thing?"

Keller sneered and thought about the question, but opted to try to figure out other choices. "Do you know these woods?"

"Well, I have lived here a couple of years, but I know them well enough. Why?"

He grabbed her again and began to drag her along. "You're going to take us to your cabins. You're going to lead the way."

"How do you know I won't trick you?" she asked.

Keller smiled and shook his head, then pointed his gun at her and cocked it. "Because I'll blow your head off and leave your brainless corpse right here in the snow, that's why."

Donna shook her head, shrugged, and replied, "Then let's hit the road. You're a special kind of dumb, aren't you?"

With that, he gave her another hard smack to the head, and the two of them began the long, snowbound journey back to Virginia Trailhead Cabins, and her sure demise.

But Donna Welk was past the point of caring now; Donna Welk had gone numb inside, and it had happened that fast.

R.W.K. Clark

CHAPTER 13

Rick Welk had been waiting for what seemed like hours for his wife to return with the simple bag of groceries she had left to purchase on the snowmobile. Eggs, a loaf of bread, a gallon of milk, and a container of coffee. At first, he had done a bit of plowing in the resort parking lot, then settled into the office on one of the lobby couches and began to read an old magazine; he hated the rag, but he had read everything else in the place, and it didn't look like the mail was going to be coming with fresh periodicals for a day or two.

He knew that the roads were bad, but one thing he could say about Donna, she could handle a snowmobile like a true professional. As a matter of fact, for such a small woman, he would be willing to put his money on her in a competition. The thought of her maneuvering that thing around like it was nothing brought a smile to his face. She was fine, and she'd be back before he knew it. In the meantime, he'd find something to do; maybe he'd even take a little nap on the lobby couch.

So, he had settled in with the magazine and read the senseless thing from cover to cover, even getting into a couple of articles about some celebrity who seemed to be nothing but a lowlife cheat, but who was he to say. Regardless of what the guy was really like in life, the magazine seemed to make him out to be nothing but a brute. He also read about a girl who had lost her leg to a shark while surfing; she had just had her first child, and that story interested Rick more than anything. It was more than amazing to him how people could go through the worst of experiences and come out stronger than ever. The human spirit was a powerful thing.

By the time he tossed the magazine on the coffee table in front of the lobby couch, he felt exhausted, like he needed a nap. He started to doze, and even fell into a light, dreamy sleep. Suddenly, he jerked awake. What time was it, and how long had he been napping? Glancing at the clock, his stomach lurched; Donna had been gone for more than two hours! What could she be doing? Donna was one of the most responsible women he had ever known, next to his mother, and now he was worried to the core. Had she crashed on the snowmobile? Had she gotten herself stuck in a good snowdrift? There were certainly plenty of them around, and they were still getting deeper by the minute. Rick wasn't sure if he should wait for her a bit longer, or take off on his own snowmobile and try to track her down. It didn't take him long to decide; he quickly bundled up, locked up the office, and headed out to the snow machine to go track down his wife, but not before leaving her a note.

The Virginia Trails Cabins were a mere mile-and-a half from the center of town, and the grocer's was a couple of blocks past that. He would get on the main highway, ride along the side of the snow-covered road, and head in the general direction of town. Either he would pass her, or he would find her walking. The very thought made him frantic and sick. He should have never listened to her when she insisted on going to town alone. Rick should have gone with her, or gone himself. But, she had always been able to handle stuff like this before! How was he to know?

So, he started off. On the route between the cabins and town, he saw absolutely no one, not so much as a car, a truck, a plow, or even another snowmobile. All was as still and dead as a ghost town. Rick didn't let the lack of life signs distract him. He continued on his way, and soon the sheriff's station was coming into sight. Immediately, his heart began to pound with relief.

The first thing he saw was Donna's snowmobile on the side of the road. There were no vehicles, and not even Sheriff Brown's plow truck was anywhere to be seen. He pulled over to the side of the road, just behind Donna's. He then walked towards the station; parked just outside the door was another snowmobile half covered in snow; obviously it had been there for a while. He went to the door; it was locked securely, so he peeked through the window, and what he saw took his breath away.

Donna was in some kind of serious trouble, and everything inside of him said that all of this had to do with that stranger, Elias Derringer. He didn't know what to do. He gave another look through the window to make sure neither of the bodies inside was Donna; all he could see was Bob Brown and the other one, who looked like Avery Rush. But who knew who else was in there rotting.

Looking up and down the main road for tire tracks, he could barely make out signs of them; the snow had managed to take care of all that. He jumped back on the snowmobile and went the two blocks to the Grocery; the place was dead, and all the interior lights were out. The town was completely shut down.

Finally, he pulled his cell from his coat and tried to dial up the state patrol. There was no signal whatsoever, and he screamed aloud in his frustration.

What was he going to do? The answer came to him. He would go back to the cabins, get on the Internet, and try to contact someone from the State Patrol. Jumping on the snowmobile, he sped back in the direction of the cabins as fast as the vehicle would carry him.

He had to find his wife before she ended up like the people flung dead all over the sheriff's station, if she wasn't in there already.

∞

"So, Mr. Keller. What exactly is the plan, anyway?" Donna was past the point of fear; this guy was a madman, and he was going to do whatever he wanted at any cost. Might as well stand up to him while she could.

He was silent for a second, thinking about his response. They were both freezing cold and breathing heavily, and he couldn't wait to get back to the cabins. She wasn't being any help at all, but could he really expect her to be? After all, she was aware of what he was capable of.

"Well," he began. "At first, I was going to tie up that prick of a husband of yours and show him what it's like to watch the one he loves suffer immensely. Now, however, those thoughts are beginning to bore me. I want to get back to the cabins, and I want you to get me to Donneley's Pass to pick up my train ticket to Rocky Mount. You help me do this, and I'll spare the both of you; I'll even forget that you exist. But if you don't, well, you can both count on a world of pain."

Donna didn't hesitate. "I think that sounds like a good deal; you've got my vote. But the problem is that you're a murdering prick. How can you be trusted? Well, you can't. Do you really think I believe you're going to let me live?"

He backhanded her hard and sent her flying to the ground. She ignored the blow and struggled to stand up again.

"So, how far are we from the cabins, do you think?" he asked in a normal tone of voice, almost as if he hadn't just hit her.

Donna took a deep breath and looked around. "Not far; maybe two full miles, but I think less. Just through these woods, around the rocky bend, across the stream, and over the hill. The cabins are just on the other side. I should tell you, the downslope of the hill is tricky, so we're gonna have to take it slow, or we could bury ourselves."

"Good; we'll take it easy then." He stopped and looked at her, turning her to meet his gaze. "How are you gonna get me there? To the train, I mean."

Donna looked at him as if he were retarded. "Rick has another snowmobile; I'm sure he would be glad to take you to the train just to get you out of our lives."

"He's not gonna take me, lady," Keller said angrily. "You are; get it straight. You do this right, I'm telling you, I won't hurt you, and you'll be home by nightfall. Got it?"

"Got it." She knew better. This guy would not let her drop him off for a train and leave her alive. He wouldn't risk her calling the cops right away, which is precisely what she would do. She knew it, and so did he. But she could play his silly games for the time being.

The two continued to trudge along, high-stepping through the drifts and making their way to the cabins in silence. Now they understood each other, and there was no reason to have any more words. The best course of action was cooperation, and soon, Elliot Keller would be gone. Even if she and her husband ended up dead, this sick dirtball would be gone.

R.W.K. Clark

CHAPTER 14

It took Rick less time to make it back to the cabin resort than it did for him to get to town. Probably his distress was the motivating factor, but he didn't care what it was. All he could think about was getting back and trying to get online to the Virginia State Patrol.

As a matter of fact, he didn't even properly park the snowmobile. He left it askew outside the office door and ran inside to boot up the system as fast as he possibly could. As he sat, waiting for the signal to pick up and get him where he needed to be on the computer, he fidgeted, paced, and swore, trickles of sweat running down his face while his mind imagined the worst possible case scenarios when it came to the murderer and his small blond wife. Oh, what if she were dead already? What if the man had already had his way with her, and she was left, frozen solid, in a snow bank along the river somewhere?

But then, a miracle. He heard the familiar series of singsong tones that let him know he was online. The computer had been worthless for literally a day-and-a half, and now here it was, up and running, and waiting for him to tell it what to do. He rushed over to the desk and sat down, then began to furiously type in the website for the State Patrol. They were the only ones he could think of to contact; after all, the bodies of the sheriff and the deputy's wife were sprawled, grotesque and dead, down at the station. There was no one else to turn to.

The computer was moving very slow, and more than once he was convinced it was going to kick him offline but good. At last, the site to the State Patrol came up, and he searched feverishly for a way to send a message, but all he could find was a 'contact us' option. He used it, writing as detailed a message as he could with the number of characters allowed. When he was finished, he pushed send, then began to search for a way to call nine-one-one online. He knew it could be done, because he heard about using an app, but for the life of him, he couldn't seem to find any of the information he was looking for.

Then he found a link that explained how to do it. Clicking on it, he breathed a sigh of relief, sat back, and waited for the slow connection to complete its course. It was right then, at that very second, that all the power to the cabin resort failed, and everything went black but for the sky outside, which was still hauntingly white.

"No! No, Not now!"

Rick swung his arm at the desk. Jumping up, he began to pace frantically. He was so distraught that he couldn't even figure out what he should do next. Finally, he did the only thing he knew to do: he coated up and left the office, leaving the office door unlocked in case Donna returned. Rick would go to any and every door he could until he found some kind of help. He would ride that snowmobile all the way to the next county if he had to, but he was going to find his wife. If that slime ball guy was still with her, he was going to tear him limb from limb.

Rick started the snowmobile for the second time that day and sped out of the snow-covered lot, his mind and heart both racing from the terror of the unknown.

∞

Donna Welk walked silently, high-stepping through the drifts as they came to the top of the hill before they would get to the cabins. Keller had a death grip on her arm, and he was pointing the gun at her back with his other hand. He hadn't said a word in a while, but as soon as the cabins came into view, she braced herself for him to start running his mouth.

"Good girl, Donna," he said, and she could hear the smile he was wearing on his face in the tone of his voice. "You know, you keep being so helpful, you might just live through all of this, but on second thought, I doubt it."

"What do you mean?" she asked. She actually had convinced herself that he was going to let her live if she drove him to Donneley's Pass. "You said –"

"I know what I said," Keller replied. "But it wouldn't do to have you take me to the train, then turn around and notify the cops of my whereabouts. I can get to the Pass myself, without your help, you know. Having a little fun with you and that husband of yours is starting to sound like the most intelligent and logical thing to do, considering it might be my last chance to have a little party."

Her heart sank, but she didn't respond. Just as she knew, he was full of it. Donna refused to let him know that she was feeling any kind of fear or despair. She wanted him to believe that she was in complete control of her emotions, even though she certainly didn't feel that way. But she wasn't going down without a fight, he'd better know it. If she was going to die, Donna Welk was going to take a great big chunk of this jerk with her.

"Have you been a sick liar your entire life?" she asked. "I suspect someone made you this way, this really didn't just happen, I'm sure. I hate your guts, but I feel bad for whatever you went through." She stopped and looked him in the eye. "I still wish you were dead, though, Keller. You're like a horse with a broken leg."

He ignored her, but his rage was building.

As they neared the cabins ever so slowly, Keller walked oblivious to anything but the fact that the roads were still devoid of traffic and piled high with snow. Not only was it still dumping from the sky, but the high winds were creating drifts as high as small houses. All Elliot Keller could do was take solace in the fact that this meant a day, two at the very most, to have his way with these two, Donna and Rick Welk. It would be a lot like his time in the cabin in the wood with those four kids, only better, because the weather would keep them isolated long enough for him to have all kinds of fun and games. He glanced at the back of Donna's head and thought about how it would feel to pull her hair out in great chunks, tearing her scalp off with it. It gave him a partial erection just thinking about it.

They reached the crest of the hill, then slowly made their way down the steep other side, which faced the cabins. Keller tightened his grip on her arm; it wouldn't do to have her tumble head over heels down the hill, only to get up, run, and escape. After all, she knew the area much better than he did.

"I have this gun on you," he said loudly over the whining winds. "Just keep walking and cooperating, and you'll be fine… at least for now."

Oh, how Donna wanted to turn around and cave his face in. She wanted to disable him and cut off his member, or better yet, shoot him right between the legs and leave him there in pain to freeze to death. Maybe it would even be just as good to take away his power over her now. She could turn around and start to fight with all of her might; he would surely put a bullet in her then and end this nightmare. But what about Rick? How she hoped that Rick was there, waiting. But she knew better; like Keller, she was paying attention to her surroundings as well, and there were a couple of things that didn't look good at all.

For one thing, his snowmobile was not in sight, and from where they were on the hill, she should have seen it clearly, parked right in front of the office. He was gone, and that was good; maybe she could stall this bottom-feeder and save her husband's life, if nothing else.

The other thing she took note of, and it was the most frightening of all, was the fact that not a single light was on, anywhere, in any home or building that she could see. Even the tall neon sign which boasted

Virginia Trailhead Cabins was out, and there was no light on in the office, either. From what she could see, there was no power whatsoever in Thompson Trails, and that was very bad indeed.

It was also obvious to Keller that Thompson Trails was in the middle of a complete power outage; he, on the other hand, found it to be one of the best strokes of luck so far. There would be no calls, no Internet, no nothing. Just time to warm up and have the fun he had been fantasizing about for hours, nothing but peaceful screaming and flowing blood. Oh, it would be good.

As they neared the foot of the hill, Keller gave her a hard shove, just for amusement. Donna tripped over her own feet and fell face-first into two feet of snow. She felt her nose hit something hard beneath the snow, and warm blood immediately began to gush from her nose. Keller watched her, smiling, as she struggled to her hands and knees, then just as she stabilized herself to stand, he planted a firm kick to her stomach, knocking the wind out of her and sending her into the snow once again. He began to laugh hysterically.

When Keller finally got control of himself, he observed her finally getting to her feet. He wouldn't kick her again, even though he was tempted, but there was really no more time to waste at this point. He had to control himself so they could get to the cabins

safely and unnoticed. But there was one thing that
bothered him as she stood; even with the wind
knocked out of her and the blood all over her face and
hair, she was smiling. There was even blood on her
teeth, from a busted lip. Her grin unsettled him a bit,
and he had to take control back quickly.

"You know, the sight of blood is visually erotic to
me," he said sarcastically as he grabbed her arm and
pushed her along violently once again. "Can't wait to
get a little relief; that nosebleed of yours is proving to
be nothing but a tease. Your husband is going to love
what I do to you, lady."

Donna shivered, but continued to walk, and she
didn't give him any sort of reply or reaction. What
would be, would be. There was absolutely no reason
for her to give him anything more to enjoy. He would
have to entertain himself with their deaths, because
she wasn't going to help him at all.

"So, since you like to do nothing but brag about
your grotesque sexual prowess, why don't you man up
and tell me a bit about all this great stuff you are going
to do to me." She smiled at him again, and this time
she added a wink. "You don't know me at all; for all
you're aware of, I might just love it."

Donna was seriously beginning to freak him out,
and she was moving a bit too fast for his taste. He was
going to make her good and dead, but now it wasn't

just about the sex and violence; now it was also about the fact that she was starting to scare him, and he didn't scare easily.

"Slow down," Keller told her, his eyes frantically taking in everything around them. "We're going to come up behind the place, by the picnic benches by the lake. I don't want anyone else to notice either one of us, especially your old man."

Keller hadn't taken notice of the fact that Rick's snowmobile was nowhere in sight. He thought her husband was somewhere in the cabins, and that was fine with him. At first, Donna had thought about leading him around in front of all the security cameras which Rick had strategically placed around the property when they first purchased the cabins, but it would be pointless now; the power was out, and the cameras were useless. She would cooperate with his plan until she could come up with something that might buy her, and her husband, some time. No matter where he had gone, he would be back soon. She knew that Rick was sick to death about her, and if he had gone to the sheriff's office for any reason, he would be fully aware of what kind of trouble she was really in.

"Go to the right," Keller shouted in the wind, jerking her hard in the intended direction. "We'll come up from behind, and then we'll go around the far end and come around by the office. He's probably in there right now, just waiting for you to come back and make him something to eat, the worthless prick." He paused. "Speaking of which, I'm starving. Make me something when we get there."

Keller hadn't been paying attention at all; Donna had been going for groceries when he grabbed her up. Well, she could make him a peanut butter on bread heels, because that was all they had. Or she could let him have free reign of the snack machine. They might even have a couple beers in the fridge in their own cabin. It didn't matter; she would be able to buy time easily enough if he was hungry. Hunger could throw a man off that much she knew.

Obediently and quietly, Donna did as he told her, and the two of them crossed the back area of the cabins, then rounded the corner and came out right in front of the office. Donna automatically reached out and grabbed the handle, and the door opened right away, struggling against the snow that had drifted up against it.

Before she could enter the dark office, Keller gave her arm a violent jerk. "Wait... why is it so dark everywhere? Why doesn't your guy have any lights on? Most of all, why is the door unlocked if he isn't in here?"

Donna smirked and shook her head. Gesturing up at the dark neon sign, she replied sarcastically, "Obviously, the power is out, ya think? I was supposed to be getting groceries, Keller. You're not as smart as you think, are you?"

He slapped her hard with his gloved hand, snapping her head around and to the side. She closed her eyes and ignored the pain that seemed amplified and explosive, thanks to her frozen face. Keller continued to look around at the stillness of the cabin area, and the fact that there was absolutely no one in sight, and he could hear the sound of no vehicles, snowmobile or otherwise.

"He isn't even here, is he Donna?" he finally asked. "He must be out looking for you. Quick, let's get inside."

The two entered the office, and Donna stopped to lock the door with her set of keys.

"Good thinking, babe; I like you more and more all the time. You might be a keeper." Keller said as he looked around. "We need candles, or lanterns, or something. What do you have?"

Donna dug blindly through the top drawer of the desk, feeling her way, until she identified a box of stick matches. Walking over to the plate glass window, she turned to Keller. "There is a box of emergency tapers in the bottom drawer of the filing cabinet, along with a flashlight."

Keller actually listened to her and went to the file cabinet. "Sure wish I had remembered to bring that Maglite from the pickup. Oh, well. This will do." He flipped on the flashlight, found the box of tapers, and took them to Donna, who proceeded to light them, one at a time, then melt the bottom and stick them to the counter; it was all she could think of to do.

"There," Keller said with relief. "Much better." He walked over to the small mini-fridge and opened it up; there was nothing inside but bottled water, and it was warm. "There's nothing here."

Donna noted that his voice was edgy, and she knew that his hunger was taking over. "Listen, Mr. Keller. Our cabin is right over there." She pointed out the window to the last cabin, which had its back to the main road. "We have a kitchenette in there, and I'm sure I can scrounge up something, even if it's a can of soup or something."

The criminal thought about it for a minute, then gave one last thorough look outside. "Okay. But I'm not crossing the lot because I have a feeling Rick's coming back soon. It wouldn't do to have my little daydream with you two ruined because a confrontation happened right in the parking lot. We'll walk around back again, then slip between the two closest cabins and enter yours. Ready? Let's go."

He grabbed her arm, and they basically reversed their previous route. Soon, they were slipping between cabins eight and nine, and in no time, Donna was unlocking the door and they were going in. She secured it behind them, then fished a heavy-duty flashlight, which was hooked to a massive battery, out from under the bed. Turning it on, she turned to Keller, who was peeking out the window.

"What's wrong?" she asked, noticing the odd look on his face.

Keller snorted and continued to stare out the slit in the curtains. "We left the candles on over there; did you do that on purpose, you conniving little wench?"

Now she was getting pissed. "I forgot all about them. What am I supposed to do when you're pushing me around all the time? I mean, a person can't think when you're rattling their brains, Einstein."

He quickly flashed her a look. "I'm going to burn that attitude out of you. Something your husband should have done before he ever hooked up with your lippy mouth. But for now, you're likely a little bit right. Can't think too clear when you're battered senseless."

R.W.K. Clark

CHAPTER 15

Earlier, Rick Welk took off from the Virginia Trails Cabins on his snowmobile, the power out, and no way to call for help regarding the state of the sheriff's office and his missing wife. He had been filled with nothing but ups and downs, fears and mental torments that Rick, until that day, had never conceived in his mind.

First, he began to go from house to house, starting with the very closest one to the resort. He received answers at every residence, but none had phones, either landlines or cellular devices, to let him use. As per what he felt to be his duty, Rick filled them in on all that he had found, the situation with Donna, and the town's desperate need of police assistance as soon as possible. He told them all about the murderer, and suggested that they refuse entrance to anyone to who might try to seek refuge from them... nothing, and he meant nothing, good would come of any such visit at the current time. They agreed to call the state patrol as soon as the power was restored.

Rick approached another house. It was the Martins'. Through the window he could see a pretty woman in her mid-thirties, crocheting or knitting or something. A man about the same age was stoking the fire, and a beautiful young girl of about fifteen was playing on a phone and munching popcorn from a big bowl.

Rick walked up onto the porch, and knocked on the door. In seconds, Jake Martin opened the door, gave him a once over, and then smiled. "Rick, how are you?" Jake seemed pleasant enough, at least for now.

Rick just smiled.

"Can I help you, son?" Jake asked.

"Yes sir," Rick replied. "Could I have a word with you alone?"

"Ah yes, come in, let me get my coat." Jake looked at his wife, who nodded kindly. "Would you like some coffee?"

Rick shook his head, "Please, would you have a cup to go perhaps?" He smiled at the pretty young girl, who smiled back shyly.

"Do you have cell service?" Rick asked the girl.

She nodded 'no'.

After a minute Janet Martin returned with an old coffee mug, "Here you go, don't worry about the mug," Janet said, as she touched Rick's frozen hand.

"Well, thank you," he replied.

The door opened behind Rick and a cold gust filled the air; there stood Jake all ready to go. "Ok, Rick, let's step outside." Jake Martin closed the door behind them.

Rick proceeded to fill Jake in on the horrid details.

Rick also stopped by the sheriff's office for the second time, hoping that all he had seen through the window there had been nothing but a nightmare. To his dismay, all of it was just as he had left it, and his heart was grieved by all that was happening in beloved Thompson Trails.

Rick sat down on his snowmobile in the blizzard which was continuing to cover the town. He put his head in his hands, feeling like a baby whose mother was nowhere to be found. All he could think about was his sweet Donna, the soft, kind, understanding woman who seemed to trust everyone she met all too much. The woman who had gone through so much grief and pain, and couldn't bear to put another through the same. Oh, Donna, who he felt such an overwhelming need to protect and serve every day of his life. Now, he could do nothing for her.

After taking a moment to pull himself together, Rick Welk took off and quickly made his way to the home of Sheriff Bob Brown and his motherly wife, Rose. Rick had no idea what he was going to say, but he had to figure it out quick.

After all, in a town the size of Thompson Trails, you were always two-blocks from everywhere.

∞

Captain Russell Johnson of the State Patrol was popping antacids like candies, and he was pacing around his office with sweat trickling down from his armpits as though a spigot had been turned on full-force.

Suddenly, the man stopped and picked up his phone. He tried once again to dial the number to the Sheriff's Office, where Elliot Keller was supposedly being held, but to no avail; their lines were still down in Thompson Trails. Slamming the receiver back into the cradle, Russell popped another antacid into his mouth, and his mind began to panic. He really shouldn't be worrying, considering the fact that he had been told the man was securely held in the jail there. But the fact was, his gut was in knots over it, and for good reason.

Since speaking with Deputy Darren Rush in the wee hours of that morning, and basically confirming the fact that they had a suspect matching Elliot

Keller's description in custody, he had heard nothing in return, not even a call to question when they would be arriving to pick up the suspect for transfer. Nothing from the Deputy, and nothing from the Sheriff. This was not a surprise in the slightest; the fact was, the power and phones were down for miles. The County had lost all of their resources shortly after that initial call.

Now Russell's phones and computers were back up and running at the State Patrol's office. But the lack of contact on the part of the Sheriff was not what had Russell Johnson on the edge of the seat, forming an antacid addiction.

The problem plaguing Johnson was simple, but horribly burdening, nonetheless. The central communications division of the State Patrol, received a computer-generated nine-one-one from a service that typically went unused.

The attempt originated in Thompson Trails. It was then, according to information provided by the Appalachian Power Company, that the town of Thompson Trails lost all power within seconds of the nine-one-one attempt.

Something was very wrong, and as far as he could think, there was only one thing he could do about it.

Finally, Russell Johnson left his office and walked up the hall to the office of a detective named Jack

Fowler. Jack was a simple, down-to-earth detective who mostly worked shoplifting and paper crimes, like forgeries and bad checks. But Detective Fowler was special in one solitary way: he moonlighted during the evening hours by driving a massive plow truck around the side streets and school routes of the County, as well as the roads going around, and leading to, Virginia Max. The good news was, it was two in the afternoon, and even though the snow was still blanketing everything in that area of Virginia, Jack Fowler had driven his plow to work, to save time, just like he did every winter.

Captain Johnson reached Fowler's door and saw him scribbling away at some unknown paperwork; this type of day was always the perfect time to catch up, but right then, Johnson didn't care about how far behind Fowler might be. He didn't even knock on the man's door. Turning the knob, he walked right in.

"Sorry to bug you, Fowler," he blurted out. "We have something of a situation in Thompson Trails regarding one escaped Elliot Keller, and I need you, or I need your plow. So which is it going to be?"

Fowler looked up at the captain with a smile on his face. "Fill me in on the details on the way, and will you bring coffee?"

"Deal, but we have to have backup on our tail," Johnson agreed. "Get your act together, and I'll gather up the boys."

"Ok, I will meet you out front, Cap." Fowler jumped to his feet.

R.W.K. Clark

CHAPTER 16

Rick had planned to make one final stop: at Sheriff
Brown's residence. Deep in his heart he was hoping
that he would knock on the door and old Bob would
answer it and start lecturing him on being out in the
elements when he should be home with Donna. Rose
would invite him in for coffee, and he would tell then
what he saw through the station window. Bob would
suggest that Darren and Avery had decided to 'get it
on' on top of one of the desks, and now they were fast
asleep. The three of them would sip their coffee and
laugh and laugh.

Unfortunately, Rick sat on the snowmobile in front
of the small yellow bungalow. The lights were out
inside, but he could see that a fire was burning brightly
in the fireplace, and several candles were lit here and
there. He could see no one moving about inside,
which led him to assume that whoever was in there
was either napping or eating a bite in the kitchen. Rick
was scared to death to knock on the door, petrified

that Bob was, indeed, one of the people dead in that office. He didn't know if he could face Rosie at all.

Finally, he bucked himself up and got off the snow vehicle. He left it running, and treaded his way through the drifted snow that obliterated the sidewalk leading to the front door. He couldn't even make out any footprints that Bob would have left behind when he left that morning.

He stood on the porch and stared at the door for longer than he would have liked to. Mustering all the courage he had in his body, Rick reached out and knocked, Rosie's pleasant voice announced that she was coming.

The very sound of her sweet voice was enough for Rick to change his mind. He could no more tell her about what he had seen through the station window than fly. Besides, he wasn't even sure himself anymore. What if it wasn't Bob in there, and Bob had gone with his truck and plow to get some kind of help at the next town. What if all the cold and confusion had messed with his mind. No, Rick wouldn't say a word. As a matter of fact, he was going to act as normal as possible, if he could, anyway.

The door locks slid out of their places, and Rosie Brown opened the door with a beaming smile. "Richard! What in the world are you doing out in this mess? Come in here right away! I have some coffee on the gas stove in my old percolator. Let's warm you up!"

She grabbed him by the arm and pulled him inside, where he stood and stomped the snow from his boots and removed his coat. "Now, don't you give a fret about taking off them boots. Just come on into the kitchen and sit down for a bit. To what do I owe the pleasure of your visit on this horrid day? You seem a bit off, Rick. What's going on?"

Rick smiled at her, but it didn't even come close to touching his heart. "Oh, not much. I see that Bob's gone; is he up at the station dealing with the mess around here?" He had to change the subject, and he had to do it now.

Rosie put a piping cup of java in front of him, along with an old green sugar container and a teaspoon. "Yeah, well, you know they were putting up that stranger for the night. Bob bought him a train ticket from the Pass to Rocky Mount, and he was going to pick him up and drive him to catch the train. Actually, I'm surprised I haven't heard from him; I mean, he hasn't even stopped by to let me know all was well. I can assume he's busy plowing people out with that big ugly beast of his."

Rick's heart sank. He sipped at the coffee, but it just made his stomach sicker. "I'm sure that's exactly what he's doing. As a matter of fact, I was stopping by to see if he'd clear my parking lot after the snow stopped. I'm guessing once the main road is clear, people are gonna be heading our way for their little romantic winter getaways."

Rosie sat across from him and stirred some sugar into her own cup. "Yes. I always loved the thought of a winter escape with my Bob, but with his job and all…"

"I know, Rose," he said. "I know."

The older woman studied him, concern in her eyes. "Are you all right, Richard? You look white as a ghost? Is Donna okay? Is she sick?"

He shook his head and faked yet another smile. "She's fine. She took off for the store for some staples, but of course, nothing's open. I left before she got back to check on the other townsfolk, so I'm guessing she's home and warm by now."

"Well, son. You'd better drink that up and get home to her, or she'll have your hide if you make her worry too much."

He nodded and drained the cup, standing and giving a stretch for good measure. "Thanks for the coffee, Rose. Tell Bob to get a hold of me, will you?"

"Of course, son."

The woman walked him to the door, then stood at the picture window and watched as he climbed on his snowmobile and took off. A block away, Rick stopped again, and buried his head in his arms and cried. He couldn't be the bearer of bad news. She would have died in front of him. He couldn't bring his heart to tell her. Oh, this thing was going to kill Rose when it all came out; it was already killing Rick.

Thompson Trails needed desperate help, and they needed it now.

As Rick rode away on the snowmobile, she kept her eyes on him until he was out of sight. Something was wrong, she knew it in her soul, but she couldn't put her finger on it. Nothing that came out of Rick Welk's mouth matched the look on his face, but she had never been one to force anyone to talk if they didn't want to. But she was worried enough to try to get a hold of Bob again.

The house phone was dead still, and Rosie didn't keep a cell. The Internet was still down, so that was useless too. Rose Brown stood at the picture window, wrapped in an afghan, and stared out for any sign of life that might come into view. But deep in her heart, she felt nothing but death and despair.

Nothing.

∞

Captain Russell Johnson rode shotgun in the massive plow truck driven by Detective Jack Fowler. As they drove, an old country song played low on the radio, but neither of them was listening to it. Jack was too busy clearing the roads for the troopers and their trucks that were following behind. All of the vehicles were taking the winding roads at very responsible speeds; sure, this was an emergency, but the point was, it would do no one any good if all of them were killed on the way to save the day.

"Are you sure that the Sheriff has this dirtbag?" Jack asked for the tenth time.

Johnson groaned and nodded. "If I told you once, I told you a thousand times: Deputy Rush told me they had a vagrant matching his description perfectly, tattoos and all. I wouldn't think nothing of it, but an online nine-one-one came through, then disconnected. There's no reason for that coming from Thompson Trails, except for the fact that they have a multiple murderer in their custody. Something happened, Jack, so stop making me repeat myself, will you?"

"I just don't want to get there and find out we all over-reacted."

Captain Johnson flashed him a look. "I don't over-react, Jack."

The men continued on in silence, pushing the snow and clearing the way for all their back up. Johnson glanced at the clock on his cell phone; there was no signal now. "At this rate, we should be there in an hour."

"Well, if you're right, I hope an hour is enough time before this monster continues to make history." Fowler had a sick look on his face, and a voice to match.

Johnson fought a frustrated tear. "I swear, threat or not, I'm gonna put this rabid dirtball out of his misery if I get the chance."

The men continued on, with no more words for the time being.

R.W.K. Clark

CHAPTER 17

Things at the Virginia Trails Cabins had not improved in the slightest. As a matter of fact, aside from Elliot Keller filling up on peanut butter by the spoonfuls and a box of old, outdated cookies, his mood had done nothing but get worse. In Donna Welk's opinion, he was doing more than psyching himself up for whatever sick thoughts were running through his head.

He had tied her to the bed, and he had done a cruel job of it, to boot. Keller hadn't used rope or twine; instead, he had opted for some thick, braided metal wire that Rick had used to secure the rental canoes to the docks. Keller found it along with bolt cutters just strong enough to cut the lengths he needed. The thought of drawing blood from her soft porcelain-toned skin excited him beyond belief, but more than that, the thought of her powerless husband watching him having fun while she bled turned him on all the more.

"Where did your man go?" he asked as he secured her painfully to the bed posters. "Maybe he decided you weren't worth coming back for. Maybe he thinks that you roped him into buying this dump, and now he's sick of the debt and heartache you're causing him with your pipe dreams."

Donna said nothing; she simply stared at the ceiling, the expressions on her face consisting of the winces that he produced when he tightened the wire.

"Nothing to say, huh, little bird?" Keller laughed and ran a length of wire around her midsection, pulling it tightly and securing it to the frame on the underside of the bed. She could swear it was cutting through her clothing and into her skin, but she was bleeding already at the wrists, neck, and ankles. Nothing he did to her now would matter. Donna Welk had resigned herself to the fact that she was going to die, and she didn't care.

"Well, he'd better hurry up," the man continued. "I'm running over to the shed to see what kind of fun toys I can find. I saw a cool saw in there that ought to make this the game of the century."

Elliot Keller was sitting next to her on the bed when he said this, and he was smiling down at her. She met his eyes, disgusted, and he caught it; it amused him even more. Bending over her, he winked and ran his tongue from her chin to her forehead. Her stomach lurched in disgust; the smell of his rotten breath reminded her of excrement, but she kept her self-control.

Sitting back up, he winked again. "See you soon, love."

With that he left, but he made a fairly big mistake. Elliot Keller had been wearing an all-purpose tool on his belt loop, a silver one with many little gadgets and knives. When he stood to leave, the tool had caught on a tear in the quilt Donna was lying on, and it popped free of the belt loop. He left unaware of his mistake.

It was inches from her, and she had to find a way to get it.

She began to squirm her hands around in the wire binds, but this resulted in doing nothing more than cutting deeper and deeper into her flesh. Blood ran down her arm, and though it was painful, it was of strange benefit. The blood greased up her arm, and pain or not, suddenly, her small right hand slid from the bind ripping her skin wide open.

Quickly, almost in a panic, she grabbed the tool and used her mouth to open the cutters; unfortunately her hand was hurt so bad she couldn't squeeze the cutters hard enough to cut through the wire. After struggling a bit with the cutters, she resorted to using her mouth to open up the large knife which was tucked away inside. When she heard the lock snap into the open position, she tucked it under her body, then proceeded to fight her wrist back into the wire binding. It hurt worse to put it back than it had to remove it, but she was past caring. The pain she felt would be nothing compared to what he planned to do with her.

Donna hoped that Rick didn't return. She knew this guy's history, and he liked to make the men watch the horrific acts he would commit against those the men cared for. Rick didn't deserve it, and she would rather die than have him see such things. Donna shook her head to rid it of the thoughts, then looked at her arm; the blood was dripping down to her elbow now, but it looked like it was slowing. She took a deep breath, and went to a safe, secret place in her mind.

Not ten minutes later, the door flew open and Keller stepped inside. He carried a saw and a rusty old machete that Rick used to cut twigs for fires during the spring and summer months. She didn't want to think about what he intended to do with them, but she could imagine, and once again, she escaped to the confines of her mind.

That was when the snowmobile came; Rick had returned.

Keller turned back to the window. "Well, will you look at that? Mr. Rick Welk is here; looks like he's ready to join the party. But he's going to have to find us first."

Donna groaned inside. She had hoped against hope that wouldn't happen. She had prayed that someone would come and save the day, but now she was sure how this story was going to end. Prayer hadn't done a thing for her; imagine that.

Donna's heart began to pound with both hope and fear. Hope that now they had a chance for survival; fear that they likely had no hope whatsoever considering who they were dealing with. What were they going to do? Keller was ready for Rick; he had plenty of wire cut, a chair positioned strategically across from where she lay bound, and a small pile of safety pins, for whatever reason. He also had a roll of duct tape, and to her, its use was pretty self-explanatory.

She and her husband were going to die today.

Keller was peeking out through a small slit in the curtains. "He's going to the office," he said with a chuckle. "Maybe it was good that we left those candles on; he's sure to know you're here now. Just think, in minutes the real fun and games will begin." He turned to her and grinned, his black, rotting front teeth repulsing her. "Are you as excited as I am, Donna Welk?"

"Oh, don't you just know it."

Keller continued to watch out the window, and soon said, "Here he comes, Donna." He rushed over and slapped a strip of duct tape over her mouth, then grabbed the flashlight he took from the office, ignoring the large one that was lighting up the cabin. Keller positioned himself behind the cabin door, looked at Donna, and held a single finger to his lips to signify silence.

Donna fastened her swollen eyes on the door, and in a few seconds, the knob turned and in stepped her husband. He instantly froze at the sight of her, panic filling his eyes. Donna tried to signify that Keller was behind the door, but Rick was so traumatized by the sight of his wife that he didn't notice. He rushed in toward her, and Keller stepped out like lightning, hitting the man in the head with all his might. With a loud 'ooof,' Rick collapsed to the floor, completely unconscious.

Keller grinned again. "You two are way too easy. Well, on to phase two, wouldn't you say?"

∞

Captain Johnson, Jack Fowler, and half of the State Patrol were just entering the Thompson Trails town limits. The panic in Johnson's stomach was tangible, and he wanted to puke, but there was no time for weakness. He would have plenty of time to get sick later.

"Where to, Boss?" Fowler asked.

"The sheriff's office," he replied stiffly. "It's right along this main drag, that much I know. This town's not very big. It will be on the left, about two more blocks."

All of the other trucks and the cops who drove them, were moving along in silence. No lights, no sirens, nothing. The last thing Johnson wanted to do was incite panic in this tiny town; all he wanted to do was make sure that his suspicions were either correct, or wrong, whatever the case may be.

"There it is, the one with the buried snowmobile."

Fowler pulled the plow over. The other vehicles pulled up single file behind the plow. Johnson got on the radio.

"No one get out; the place looks dead. Fowler and I are going to approach and investigate the scene."

The two men crawled out of the big plow truck, guns drawn, and approached the building. Fowler immediately tried the door, but Johnson went right to the window. Suddenly, he could no longer hold down all the coffee he had ingested during the drive; he bent over and puked all over the pure white snow, melting it like salt in water.

"Are you okay, man?" Fowler asked. "What is going on in there?"

Johnson wiped his mouth on the sleeve of his coat. "Dead. They're dead in there, and it's a bloody mess. Have the men get the battering ram out. We have to get in there now."

It took no time for the men to beat the door in; three solid hits, to be exact. The door gave way like paper on the third hit, and all the men went tumbling inside. The smell of blood was overwhelming, and three of the troopers had to go outside to up their own coffee and donuts.

Fowler turned to Johnson. "That's the sheriff there, isn't it? Who's the woman?"

"I'm not sure. Let's clear the perimeter and make sure there are no other victims." Johnson barked to all the officers.

"Fowler. Get on the police radio; we need a bus, or two or three. Get the coroner here, and as many cops as possible. Set up roadblocks, no one gets in or out. Notify the feds. We can only hope this sick scumbag hasn't gone too far, and we can only hope he's alone."

Unfortunately, they were all dead. The deputy was found in the far back closet. On the floor near where the girl lay splayed wide open, was a broken framed photograph, probably dropped from the desk during the confrontation. The photograph verified she was the deputy's wife, and she had been horribly brutalized.

"Get a blanket out of that closet," Johnson directed the officers milling around, "Let's give this girl some dignity."

Fowler came running in. "We've got two busses coming from Donneley medical center and more backup on the way. They'll meet us here."

One of the officers returned with two blankets, which he used to cover the sheriff and the young woman. Johnson turned to Fowler and said, "We're going to find the sheriff's widow." He turned to the others. "All of you wait here, unless I call for you. We have to find Mrs. Brown and try to figure out our next step."

With that, the two men left in the plow after tracking down the sheriff's address in the small Thompson Trails phone book. Both men dreaded the job they were about to do, but it had to be done. It was all they could do to hope that she might have some unknown bit of information that would give them some kind of idea where Elliot Keller might be.

R.W.K. Clark

CHAPTER 18

It was so hot that the heater had to be pumping out at a hundred degrees. Rick squirmed a bit, trying to kick the blankets off his feet, but no matter how hard he tried, they remained covered and sweaty, causing the rest of his body to feel as though he were dying from some kind of fever. He groaned; why did he feel so weak? He couldn't even seem to muster the energy to climb out of bed and adjust the thermostat.

He was trying to say Donna's name, but his voice sounded muffled and low. Slowly, he became aware that there was a reason for this; something was covering his mouth, something was keeping him from speaking.

Rick's eyes began to flutter, rapidly at first, then slower, until he had them open all the way. He was confused, and his head was pounding. He wasn't in his bed at all; he was sitting in one of the chairs in his own cabin. Not only was he sitting in it, he was wired to the thing, or so it appeared. As he fought to clear his own vision, he could see blood trickling from the wounds that the tight wire had created.

Now he looked up, and the first thing he saw brought a scream from the depths of his gut, but the scream stopped at the duct tape that covered his mouth. Donna was lying on the bed, wires binding her to the posters. She was beat, or so it appeared. He could see cuts on her head that were crusted with blood, and like him, her wrists were bloody and sliced where the wires held her. She was staring at him with wide eyes, which she shifted now and then toward the bathroom.

His wife rapidly shook her head in an effort to tell him to stay quiet, but he was getting angrier and angrier with each passing second. It was all coming back to him in a rush now: the stranger he had called Sheriff Brown on, the dead bodies at the station, his attempt to get ahold of the state police over the computer that failed so miserably.

Movement from his left caught his eye, and he turned his head to see the stranger who had been the cause of all of it. Rick began to struggle against the wire, but with each movement, it just cut into his skin deeper, causing him to wince in pain.

"Uh, yeah, I wouldn't do too much of that if I were you," the man said. "Keep going and you'll do yourself in, and that would rob me of the pleasure, you see. So, sit still."

He paced between Donna on the bed and Rick in the chair, stopping after he had passed once between them. He had Rick's old rusty machete in one hand, and he was toying with the point of it with his forefinger. Rick kept his eyes focused on the guy's every move, his mind racing as he tried to figure out something, anything, he could do to save the lives of his wife and himself.

"I guess, introductions are in order, Mr. Welk," the man said. "Donna and I have gotten pretty close; she knows me, at least, she knows me better than you do. My name is Elliot Keller. You might have heard of me; most people have."

Of course, he had heard of him; the sicko was a murdering monster, but he was supposed to be in prison at the max penitentiary. How did this animal manage to get out of his cage? Rick's stomach began to tremble inside with fear; this couldn't end well. It seemed to him that the guy was planning to do to Donna what he had done to the three girls that got him sent away in the first place. He had to figure something out fast.

"I already know your name, of course," Keller continued. "I know a lot about you, Mr. Welk, and your pretty little wife." He sat down on the edge of the bed near Donna's head and shoulders, but continued to face Rick and speak. "Now, you should feel like quite the lucky one; you have a front row seat to what is going to be the second greatest show in history. The first, well, we all know about the first greatest show. This one will be close, but with just one woman, well, the entertainment factor is a bit limited."

Keller stood up and put the machete on the nightstand next to the bed. Out of his back pocket he took out a hefty pair of scissors, silver ones that Donna used for cutting material when she made the curtains for the cabins. He sat back down and took her shirt at the neck and began to cut it. Soon, it lay open, baring her milky white skin and bra. Next, Keller cut up each long sleeve, and at last, the top fell away and lay beneath her, forgotten. Rick began to go nuts in earnest, forgetting the sharp pain that the wire was causing as it tore at his flesh.

Keller stood up and began to do something of a jig. Nothing fancy, just a couple of sloppy steps here and there. He had long black hair, and he had pulled the bangs and most of the top back into a ponytail. The rest of it dangled in long, greasy strands around his face. He smiled, did a twirl, and sat down at the foot of the bed. He began to take off her pink camouflage hiking boots, which caused her to cry out through the tape. The jerking motion he made as he removed the boots deepened the cuts on her ankles, and tears were shooting out of her closed eyes.

"We are going to have a bit of fun, the three of us," he said happily as he tossed one boot to the side, pulled off her thick wool sock, and started on the next boot. "I mean, I have to be honest, I'll be having the most fun, but I'm sure you'll be entertained enough by what you see that you'll be able to admit that you enjoyed it a bit."

The other boot came off, and Keller tossed it in the same direction as the first, then removed the other sock. He stood up and took a place next to Rick, grabbing him by his hair and jerking his head up so he was forced to look at Donna.

"Open your eyes, Mr. Welk, and get a good eyeful," Keller laughed. "I know, I know, it isn't much now, but just wait until we get those jeans off."

Rick clamped his eyes shut, frustration and fury filling him up. "I said open them!" Keller punched him hard in the side of his head, so Rick did as he was told. "You know, I guess now is as good a time as any to take care of this whole eye thing now."

The man walked away, and when he returned, he stood in front of Rick and held his hand open before him. Lying innocently in the man's palm were two large safety pins. Rick looked at them, then looked up at Keller, confused.

"Oh, I see, you don't get it." Keller straddled him in the chair and sat on Rick's lap, facing him. "These are to help you so you won't be tempted to close your eyes during the good parts. Now, it's going to hurt, believe me, but the more you squirm, the worse it will be. And if you fight me, I swear, I'll do things to your wife that nightmares are made of. Well, I'm gonna do those things anyway, but I can make them completely horrible instead of just downright bad. So, sit still."

Keller placed one of the pins on the dresser directly behind Rick, then opened the other one. He wrapped his left arm tightly around the man's head to hold it in place, aimed the sharp tip of the pin at the man's eye, then paused. "This works best if you have your eyes part-way open, but you can close them if you want. I'll get the job done no matter what."

Rick knew what he was going to do, and his body wanted to fight, but his heart and mind was saturated with Donna. He bit the insides of his cheeks to prepare for the pain, which came fast. Keller stabbed the pin through Rick's left eyelid, gently yanked it open, then stabbed the pin through the man's eyebrow. Once it was all the way through the skin, he closed the pin and stood up to observe his handy work.

"Beautiful!" he gushed. "I must say, I've done this a number of times in my life, but that is one of the cleanest and most attractive pinnings I've ever accomplished!"

It hurt! Blood was running down into Rick's eye, and the burning that the pin was causing was nothing short of torment. He couldn't blink or even come close to closing the eye; he just stared at the man and let his anger and fear keep him still.

"Time for the next!"

Keller grabbed the second pin and straddled him once again. The second eye went much faster, though it hurt a lot worse for some reason. Once again, he didn't struggle or fight; Rick just groaned in pain and controlled himself as best as he could. He didn't want to do anything that would make things harder on Donna.

When Keller stood again, he fetched the scissors and danced around a bit more, humming what sounded like an old song of sorts. Scissors in hand, he pulled what appeared to be a dark blue scrub shirt over his head; that was when Rick noticed the man was wearing scrub pants as well. He was wearing clothes from the jail, and the realization made Rick want to laugh out loud.

Once the shirt was off, Keller kicked off his boots, then walked to Rick and bent down, putting his nose right against the man's. "Anyway, it's time to get back to Donna. I always loved a good game of strip murder;

looks like I'm ahead of the game so far, wouldn't you say?"

Keller stood, spun around to Donna, whose eyes were filled with horror and anger, and he held up the scissors. "I think we'll go for the bra next, what do you say, pretty lady?"

∞

Captain Johnson and Jack Fowler stood on the step of Sheriff Brown's quaint little home. They had just knocked and were waiting, soberly, for Mrs. Rose Brown to answer the door. They could both see her coming through the large picture window next to the door. She was a tiny, white haired lady, and her bubbly, friendly personality was obvious just by the way she carried herself. Fowler looked at Johnson, his eyes full of sadness; Johnson simply shook his head in return.

The main door opened, and Rose looked at the two men through the wrought iron framed screen door. The smile on her face disappeared as if by magic. Captain Johnson knew immediately that the news of her husband's death had been told in completion when their eyes first met.

"Mrs. Brown, my name is Captain Russell Johnson with the State Patrol. This is Detective Fowler." He motioned to his companion. "May we come in, please?"

The woman didn't answer, she just opened the screen and held it for them as they crossed the threshold. They both began to stomp the snow off their shoes. Rose stopped them by touching them both on the arm.

"Never mind the snow. You can have a seat if you like." She began to walk into the living room. "I believe I know why you're here."

The men followed her and took seats in matching overstuffed chairs that went with the couch and loveseat in the room. Rose sat on the loveseat, and Johnson noted that a box of tissues was located right by where she was sitting.

"Mrs. Brown, this is never easy…"

The older woman wrapped her arms around herself as if she was cold. "Men like you don't knock on the doors of people to announce things like block parties or potluck dinners at the church." She plucked a tissue, but held it in her hand. "When and how did it happen?" Tears were already running down her face.

Fowler and Johnson glanced at each other, then Johnson replied, "Very early this morning, probably around dawn."

Rose nodded. "I assume it had something to do with that vagrant he was helping."

"Yes ma'am."

More tears fell from her eyes, and she wiped them away, then straightened her shoulders and lifted her chin. "I always expected his career would end this way, but I took a bit of solace in the fact that this is such a small, safe town, you know?"

Neither of them answered; it was best to just let her talk at a time like this.

"So, who was this guy? This stranger that needed so much help?" Now her voice took on an angry edge. Her husband had gone out of his way to assist someone in need, and this had happened as a result.

This time, Fowler entered the conversation. "He was an escapee from Virginia Max. I know you haven't had power, so your husband had no idea of knowing who he was."

Johnson interrupted. "I called in the night and spoke to Deputy Rush to tell him about the escape, ma'am; we were calling every location that didn't have power. The deputy made us aware at that time that he believed he had the suspect in custody already. Unfortunately, we believe that the man overheard enough of the conversation to figure out that we were on to his location, and… Darren is dead, too."

"Does his wife, Avery, know?"

Fowler looked at his feet, so Johnson continued. "Ma'am both the deputy and his wife are deceased as well. All three were found at the station house."

Rose began to cry in earnest, and the men gave her the time she needed. She was a strong woman, though, and in less than five minutes, she blew her nose and looked at them with red-rimmed eyes. "My lord, you boys get out there and find this animal, and put him down." Her eyes were also filled with expectation, as if she knew there was more.

"Well?" she finally said. "I assume since you are still sitting here, there is a reason?"

Johnson clasped his hands together and sat forward. "Ma'am, we have several reasons to believe that the man is still in or around Thompson Trails, and we think he has a hostage. We were just wondering if you have possibly seen or heard anything that was just... out of the usual. Anything at all."

Rose thought for a minute. "I haven't left the house at all. The one person I've spoken to since Robert left for work this morning was Rick Welk; he stopped by, and I gave him a cup of coffee."

"Who is Rick Welk?" Fowler asked.

A couple of tears fell again, and Rosie wiped at them with frustration. "Rick and his wife Donna own the Virginia Trails Cabins, just on the edge of town. They usually don't go visiting, but Rick said he just wanted to check on me, to make sure I was okay." She went quiet for moment, then continued. "You know, when he came he was so... sober, you know, serious. I asked him what was wrong, but he changed his attitude up right away. Stayed for a moment, then left. You know, Robert told me that the stranger who was at the jail had been hanging around the cabins, and it was Rick who called him to come pick him up."

Now the two men exchanged long, knowing glances. "Where is the resort again, ma'am?" Fowler asked.

"Straight up the main road, that way. It's on the right; you can't miss it. About ten small cabins, with the lake right behind them. Cute little... oh, no! Do you think he's there?"

Fowler and Johnson stood up. "Ma'am, once again, we're sorry for your loss, and we wish we could stay longer, but we have to find this man. He's very dangerous."

"Of course," she replied, following them to the door. As they stepped outside, she asked. "Can I ask who this man is?"

"It's the murderer, Elliot Keller," Fowler said quietly. "Please, stay inside and keep things locked up. If your phones come on, call around and tell everyone to do the same."

"You boys put him down this time." She watched the men as they made their way to the large plow truck and climbed inside. Johnson got on the radio and called for the men at the sheriff's office.

"We're gonna need all available officers for back-up at the Virginia Trails Cabins on the north end of town, and we need them right away. We have reason to believe Keller is there with two hostages. One Donna and Rick Welk."

Fowler pulled the truck out and headed up the road. "You think he's there, huh?"

Johnson stared straight ahead, his hand on his gun. "I know he is"

R.W.K. Clark

CHAPTER 19

When Johnson and Fowler were sitting in Rose Brown's living room, Keller was finishing up with the removal of Donna Welk's clothing. The woman now lay, bound and bleeding, bare naked as the day she was born. Her husband watched, helpless and heartbroken, as blood and tears ran around his eyes and down his face. Keller, on the other hand, had a saw, the machete, and a couple of steak knives from the kitchen. He told them with amusement that he needed two because knives like that broke so easily.

In Donna's mind, it was obvious that he had forgotten the multi-purpose tool, and she wasn't about to remind him of it.

Keller turned the radio on low to a heavy metal station and walked around the bed, passing back and forth. After a moment, he said, "Now, let's play a game. I'm going to ask a series of questions, and you, Rick, are going to answer them. No need to remove the tape; they will all have yes or no answers. If you get them wrong, Donna gets a poke or a cut with one of my fun little tools. If you get them right, well, she gets a really good poke with my main tool, in the orifice of my choosing. Sound like fun?"

Rick shook his head madly and began to try and scream against the tape. Keller took up one of the steak knives and stabbed it clean through the sole of Donna's right foot. She screamed and cried, her body arching against the wire at her midsection, digging into the flesh and making her bleed more. When he pulled the knife out, the tip broke off, and was sticking slightly out of her foot.

"I said, no screaming, Rick," he said calmly.

Rick tried to calm himself, and his eyes sought out Donna's but hers were clamped shut against the pain, as tears ran down her face. If he could get his hands on this guy, he would tear the dirtball limb from limb.

"So, let's play," Keller began. "First question: the male victim who survived the cabin attack that sent me to prison; was his name Teddy?"

Rick's mind went to the more than five-year-old crime immediately, and he tried to pull up the details, but they hadn't lived there then. Sure, it had been news all around the United States, but still. Regardless, the name 'Teddy' didn't ring any kind of bell at all.

"Tick-tock, tick-tock."

Rick had to answer; he had to take a chance, even though it was a losing situation either way. He began to nod yes furiously.

"Wrong answer!"

Keller ran to the left side of the bed and plunged the broken knife into Donna's arm, then pulled it out forcefully. Another round of tears and taped-up screams came, along with a stream of blood which saturated the bed beneath her arm.

Keller ignored their screams and began to walk around the bed again. "Question number two: was I born in Georgia?"

Rick's eyes searched his face for any kind of sign that would give away the answer, but the guy was so busy smiling and dancing around that there was no way to read him. Rick watched as Keller put down the broken knife and picked up the machete, then ran his finger gently along the blade.

"Time's running out, Rick."

Rick nodded 'yes' another time.

"Wrong again! I'm a Virginia boy all the way!"

Keller took the machete and pressed the blade hard against the bare skin of Donna's right thigh. He dragged it, going deeper as he went, watching the seeping blood as it oozed down the side of her leg. Donna was getting pale, and this time she didn't scream. She whimpered, her body and mind growing weak. Rick, however, continued to holler against the tape.

Keller stopped cutting just at her ankle. "This thing's a lot sharper than it looks, isn't it? I think I'm gonna have to keep this as a souvenir."

He turned to Rick for the third time. "Question number three, and believe me, I can't wait for you to get one of these right. I am so hard that if I don't put it somewhere soon I might explode. Question three: am I an only child?"

Rick stared at him. He was sure the guy had siblings of some kind. He didn't want Donna to lose any more blood, but worse than that, he didn't want this man to rape her, and a right answer would result in just that. He knew what answer he was going to pick: he was going to nod yes, that Keller was an only child.

"Hurry up, Ricky-boy," Keller whispered in his face. "Don't want time to run out, do you?"

Rick held his breath, looked the man in the eye, and gave a firm nod 'yes'.

"Bing-bing-bing! You are correct! Finally! Time for the real stuff!"

Rick Welk began to scream through the tape once again.

∞

At the entrance to the Virginia Trails Cabins sat Fowler and Johnson in the pickup plow, with the ignition off. Four other state patrol trucks sat lined up alongside them, all with the lights out and engines off as well. They were watching the only cabin with lights creeping through the pulled blinds: the cabin that Rick and Donna Welk called home.

Captain Johnson was communicating with the men over the police band radio. The plan was to have a group, led by him, sneak around the back of the cabin and surround it while the others blocked the driveway entrance and the perimeter of the property. They were all armed, vested, locked and loaded, but they wouldn't make a move to enter until they were sure that someone was inside. So far, all they could see was the sliver of light through the drawn curtains. All it would take was a single peep, and they would barnstorm the place.

"Okay, I want all of the men I chose to fall in behind me; close none of the vehicle doors hard. We don't want him to know we're here, because we all know this animal will do something rash." Johnson looked at Fowler, who would mind the men taking care of the perimeter. "All the rest of you don't make a move without Fowler's say, got it? And boys: shoot to kill."

Ten-fours came back in unison.

Checking his gun for the hundredth time, Johnson gave one more look at the detective next to him, then got out of the vehicle and closed the door gently enough just to latch it; it barely made a sound. All the troopers who were joining him followed suit, and together, they made their way, around the back of the main office and to the rear of the Welks' cabin.

Soon, the group was at their goal, and splitting into groups, they sidled up each side of the cabin. The men stopped just out of sight along the sides of the small building, but Johnson crept, kneeling, under the window and to the door.

He didn't need to wait for long; the first thing Johnson heard were the muffle screams of pain and horror in two different voices. He heard the laughter of a single man, Elliot Keller, who sounded like he was having the time of his life. Johnson shot a look up to the sky and gave thanks that the Welks, from what he could hear, were still alive, even if they were hoping at this point that they weren't.

He looked to the left side of the cabin and made eye contact with the lead man there; then, he did the same to the right. With a jerk of his head and a pointing motion of his hand, Johnson stood, gave the door a solitary violent kick, and rushed inside, his entire team at his heels.

What they saw inside that cabin would haunt their dreams for the rest of their lives.

R.W.K. Clark

CHAPTER 20

At the same time the state troopers were discussing strategy on the police band radio, Rick Welk was correctly answering the question regarding the existence of siblings in Elliot Keller's life. As it turned out, answering the question correctly was the worst thing Rick had ever done, and now his wife Donna was being given the grand prize.

Elliot Keller had removed all of his clothing, then positioned himself on his knees between Donna's spread legs. He was laughing, and telling a story of a time he was blamed for misbehavior, and he was graphically describing the punishment he received. As he did so, Keller held a lit cigarette to various parts of Donna's body, ignoring her muffled screams, as well as those of her horrified husband.

"And now for the coup de grace," hollered with great, flamboyant gestures. With one powerful thrust, he was inside of her, and Donna was helpless to do anything but allow the rape to go on.

But instead of pumping away, Keller held his position, burned her a couple more times, then tossed the cigarette on the nightstand, where it lay burning the surface of the wood. He picked up the machete, which was lying next to Donna's thigh on the bed, then he drew back with one arm, brought it forward, and sliced a long diagonal cut from her right shoulder to the opposite hip bone. The cut began to bleed profusely, but Keller paid the blood no mind. His head was thrown back, his mouth wide open in ecstasy as his body responded to the violence that turned him on so much.

Rick began to sob helplessly, his face soaked in sweat and tears. Never had he felt so powerless as a man in his life. He wanted to die.

Donna's eyes went to her right wrist, the one she had slid out of the wire before. She glanced at Keller, and noticed he was looking up; Rick was forgotten, and so was she at the moment, but she had no idea how long that would last. Slowly, Donna pulled her arm downward through the loop. It hurt like nothing she had ever felt, and she realized that the flesh had swollen. She was passed the point of caring. She continued to pull with a bit more pressure each second, until it seemed to be blinding her. She pulled, and the blood began to flow once again, the sound of her skin ripping made her bite down hard, gritting her teeth. Her right hand suddenly slid free. Donna held it up anyway, just in case movement would make him look at her. Then, millimeter by millimeter, she put her hand down and slid it under her.

There it was: the tool with the knife out. Donna watched Keller as she wrapped her hand around its handle. With a glance at her husband, Donna mouthed the words 'I love you.'

As fast as lightning, she pulled the knife out and buried it deep in his flesh, right about his pubic hair line. Holding on with an iron grip, Donna gave the knife a yank upward cutting until the blade hit his ribs, then she jerked it down again. Blood poured from him, pouring all over her, but Donna Welk was smiling and looking at his eyes.

Elliot Keller looked back, shock and surprise written all over his face. The machete, which he had been holding in mid-air fell onto the bed behind him, and his surprise turned into anger quickly. But Donna wasted no time; she pulled the knife out and drove it into his thigh, yanked it back out, and watched an incredible stream of blood shoot across the room from his now severed femoral artery.

Keller looked down, and his hands fell limply to his sides. The man was beginning to weave back and forth, and even though he was still staring at Donna, his focus was waning. He was going to die right on top of her.

Suddenly the door flew in, as though someone had set off a bomb just outside. Policemen poured into the cabin, guns drawn, and all of them completely focused on the sick freak who still had his member buried inside Donna Welk's battered body.

Gunfire rang out and filled the room, spraying blood and brains all over the walls.

"You sick freak." Russell Johnson's voice was deadly, determined, and filled with disgusted rage. "I swear, get him off of her, now."

Rick sat frozen to the chair, his eyes wide as saucers, and the safety pins forgotten, even as they assisted him in his stare. He watched Keller closely to see what the man was going to do.

Johnson spoke through grit teeth. "No second chance this time, scumbag."

"Get him off me!" Donna screamed. "Get him off!"

The men moved faster than her eyes could register, and in seconds, they had one dead Elliot Keller, lying on the floor.

Two months later.

Donna and Rick made plans to sell the cabins. No one in Thompson Trails ever wanted to lay eyes on the place again.

ENTREATY

My creativity is fueled by readers like you. If you enjoyed this novel, I implore you to please write a review, and share your experience on the retailer's website. The livelihood for authors is fully dependent on reviews, and I must say, it is the largest obstacle as a struggling author that I have encountered. Please tell a friend, tell a loved one about this read. With your help, I will be one step closer to overcoming this obstacle. In return, I thank you from the bottom of my heart, and greatly and deeply appreciate your time and effort.

Humbled, with gratitude,
R.W.K. Clark

ADDITIONALLY

Works by R.W.K. Clark

PASSING THROUGH

ISBN-10: 1948312018 ISBN-13: 978-1948312011
ISBN-10: 1948312093 ISBN-13: 978-1948312097
ISBN-10: 1948312107 ISBN-13: 978-1948312103
ISBN-10: 1948312115 ISBN-13: 978-1948312110

Psychological Thriller

I believe that writers and novelists, as in any profession, change and grow over the timespan that they work and produce. Any of my readers and fans who are familiar with my books and the 'genres' they are 'classified' under are able to recognize the point I am making. Authors' characters get more detailed and personal; descriptions get a bit more intense, as do emotional scenes of any kind. I have also found, for myself, that with each and every book I put out, I seem to get a bit more 'guts' about what I am willing to put down on paper. For instance, I'll admit it, in the beginning, writing a detailed love scene was something I dreaded, but I do much better now, and I'm getting much more comfortable, with experience, in that particular area. This, of course, is just one example.

'Passing Through' is my latest release, and it is the third book I have written that I would call a psychological thriller. The first was 'Brother's Keeper', and when I wrote that I thought it was a bit much. 'Passing Through' is on an entirely different level, however, not just in its depth and explicitness. Now, I realize that there will be fans out there who will love this book; perhaps it will surprise them, and they will find it will be just what they were waiting for from me. Others, though, are going to despise it.

'Passing Through' was very difficult for me to write for a number of reasons, but there were two in particular that took a toll on me. First, I have had close personal experience and interactions in passing with violent criminals, and their minds and ways of thinking are ugly and burdensome; they are not people you want to make regular friends of. To put these things into words and make people understand was, well, exhausting.

I also found myself quite beaten up after writing each and every violent part. I didn't want the parts to be mild, because the character of Elliot Keller was a horrible, horrible man. It thrilled him to do the things he did to people to the point that the only motivation he had for escaping prison was to have a chance to indulge in his deviant behavior yet once more in his life. Some of the visuals I got, which are what prompt what I write, made me sick, and more than once, I had to step away and breathe.

Now, let's talk about Keller a bit better. Initially, I wrote his character with little to no explanation as to why he was the killer that he was. It didn't matter at first; to me, he was just a bad man, an animal. Many murderers never suffer wrong at the hands of another, yet they choose to harm others over and over, for no other reason than they like it and it's fun.

I changed this. The reason I began to explain a bit about what made Elliot what he was is simple: I had to show readers the ripple effect, that can literally last for centuries, when this type of violence is bestowed by one on another. What happened to Keller, Keller did to others, and it would not stop there... it would never stop. I didn't go into his past to provoke pity or compassion. He is nothing more than a rabid animal, and his actions clearly demonstrate that. With that being said, by the end of the book, you will understand what I mean, and you will still hate him all the more.

Thompson Trails, Virginia is yet another fictional town full of ignorant, innocent unawares that have no idea what is about to hit them. I love to develop these little burgs, and I enjoy creating the people who live blissfully within their boundaries. I grow to love many of the characters, no matter how brief their appearances; as readers know, authors kill people off, no matter their age or how good of a person they are. This happens a lot in Thompson Trails, and I grieved each death. But in reality, killers don't flip coins, and they don't pick and choose. Bad things happen, and they always seem to happen to good people.

Finally, I would like to touch base briefly on Rick and Donna Welk, the owners of the cabin resort, but mostly I want to focus on Donna. Donna and Rick have suffered the loss of a pregnancy, which spurred them to move and buy the cabins. On the outside, Donna is soft, kind, generous, a good wife, and wouldn't hurt a fly. She is hurting that she cannot have a child, and she is simply trying to build a new, happy life around this reality. I believe that readers are going to be surprised by the fiber this little woman is made of, and I think they will be furious at the outcome Keller causes her and the man she loves.

For those of you who are lovers of horror, well, here you go. I hope you enjoy it. I also hope it makes you as sick as it makes me, because it is that horror and sickness that makes us face the harsh realities of life and keeps us on our toes. I didn't write this and then roll it in sugar because it isn't candy; it is a jagged little pill that will slice your throat straight open if you swallow too fast. Believe me, when I say, it is not for children. Best to give fair warning; I wrote this in a manner that it would leave some kind of mark. Hopefully, the mark is a good one.

So, sit down with the lights on and enjoy the terror that is Elliot Keller in 'Passing Through'.

BROTHER'S KEEPER

ISBN-13: 978-1948312134 ISBN-10: 1948312131
ISBN-13: 978-0692744741 ISBN-10: 0692744746
ISBN-13: 978-1948312141 ISBN-10: 194831214X

Psychological Thriller

'Brother's Keeper' is my first psychological thriller, and it was simultaneously fun and difficult to write. It tells the story of Scott Sharp, a widowed traveler whose train makes a stop at the tiny town of Burdensville. Here, Scott tries to assist a waitress being harassed by a drunk and gets himself arrested, which results in pulling the stranger into the dark secrets the town holds, and the secrets won't let him go.

Writing this story was fun for a variety of reasons. It was off the beaten path compared to most books I write. The monster in this book is not a vampire, witch, or zombie; instead, the monster is an unknown man who is murdering women at night who pass through the town. Developing the character of the murderer was a good time; I wanted him to be dull, but intelligent; he needed to be needy, but in control in ways no one understood. He needed to have deep-seated issues that were in such a terrible knot that even those who might care about him didn't know how to sort them out.

Scott walks into Burdensville without the slightest idea what has been happening to this town. He is, utterly and completely, an innocent victim. When he first gets to the café and tries to protect the waitress from the town drunk, he is put under arrest by the sheriff, which is really the first sign that something is off in that town; even the other patrons in the restaurant keep their mouths closed when he implores them to tell the sheriff that he did nothing wrong. The whole place is off, and he can't seem to put his finger on what is happening around him. All Scott knows is that he's trapped in a jail cell waiting to see a judge that won't come for more than a week, but it is there that Scott himself will begin to unravel the goings-on in Burdensville for himself.

Of course, we cannot have a murder mystery without romance, even if it is slight. In the case of Brother's Keeper, I created a slow but sure relationship between Scott and the waitress he tried to save when he was arrested. In the beginning, she was aloof with him, but soon she is forced to take meals to the jail to feed Scott, and it is during this time the two get to know each other. Inevitably, they fall in love, but not before the killer puts her own sanity to the test.

Sheriff Robert Darby is keeping the most secrets in this town, as readers will discover. I chose the sheriff for this role because none of what happens in the book would be possible without the authority that his badge permits him to have. Now, some may say that the storyline in regard to him is somewhat flaky or unrealistic. I would have to tell those readers that this is fiction. The beauty of fiction is exactly what I did in the case of Sheriff Darby and his unutterable secrets.

I tried to put a bit of everything in this book: Old lady hen twins who are the gossipers of the town; Dickie, the café owner, who has great fatherly affection for Denise, and who has seen some of the craziness Burdensville truly has to offer. The town drunk, who is also mentally challenged and basically faces life alone except for the help of the sheriff; he is essential to the novel, in all of its insanity and desperation.

To put things in a nutshell for my readers, there is a past history that the sheriff is actively covering up; he is doing this for more reasons than I can explain here, but his secrets are vile, shameful, and have instilled a sense of obligation in Sheriff Darby that he can never silence. It is, quite literally, a huge burden for him, but he carries these things, and acts upon them, out of the best interest of the townsfolk as a whole, not to mention himself. Readers may feel like Sheriff Darby is something of a bad guy, but I cannot express enough that the things he does which seem so wrong are committed out of a pure heart, a heart that is trying to make things right in a situation where they will never, ever be right again. He is not the guy to hate here, though throughout the pages it clearly seems that way. The reality is, Sheriff Darby is as much of a victim as all of those who have been murdered on the outskirts of the town.

I wanted people to really be in Burdensville while they read this. I also wanted readers to get a very specific feel for the town; Mayberry without a shower. I did my best to convey the gloom of the constant shadows that seem to hang over the place, even when the sun was shining. I also wanted to make it clear that Sheriff Darby wasn't the only one feeling obligation; the entire town does. That's more or less what happens in small-town life and, evil or not, Burdensville is no different.

BOX OFFICE BUTCHER

ISBN-13: 978-0997876758 ISBN-10: 0997876751
ISBN-13: 978-1948312165 ISBN-10: 1948312166
ISBN-13: 978-1948312158 ISBN-10: 1948312158

Psychological Thriller

Box Office Butcher is a psychological thriller murder mystery about a killer who is murdering people in an identical manner as that which is done in a new hit slasher flick. While the premise is similar to that of the popular 'Scream' franchise, readers will find that I have written this in a manner that is actually much different, making it unique in almost every aspect. The bottom line, however, is the same: There is a lunatic killing people out there, and he has to be stopped.

Dubbed 'The Box-Office Butcher' by the press, the killer is committing a couple of killings every weekend, and he isn't doing this in a specific area; he's moving around. This results in Detective Kevin Harmes, of the Los Angeles Police Department, scrambling from here to there and back again to try and keep up. Fortunately, this seasoned cop has some pretty spot-on suspicions of his own. Regardless of this fact, 'The Butcher' manages to keep him on his toes, and miserably so, with the sick game he is playing.

It is important to understand that the killer has a vendetta, and it is very necessary to accomplish it. For him, these murders are rooted in a history of abuse and rage, and he feels the compelling need to take care of the issue, which he has carried around with him his entire life. It is more than simply killing because he's a sicko, or because it's fun, though these are true as well. His actions are essentially a way to make right a past that has, unbeknownst to him, destroyed him from the inside out.

Keep in mind that none of the 'copycat' killings are identical to the one from the film which they are meant to emulate. The Butcher doesn't have the kind of power it would take to make his victims cooperate with a scripted film and still enjoy the spontaneity and horror he is set on sparking and enjoying. With this being said, he is a careful planner, spending both time and money to get the real-life murders as close to the ones on film as he possibly can, and he comes terrifyingly close each time.

The Butcher is a man of means, and this becomes obvious by his ability to move so freely from city to city; obviously, he isn't broke or lacking finances of some kind. This is a point which Detective Harmes picks up on and is vital to his investigation. Unfortunately, the suspects that are on his list all fall into this category at one level or another, so he must do the footwork to weed them out.

The Butcher is a very sick man, and it was important to drive this home through a variety of methods. I wrote about him watching the scenes over and over again, which he was preparing to emulate, even though it was obvious he knew them like the back of his hand. I also added an element of sexual stimulation when he watched, as an added bonus pointing to his psychosis.

The hardest part of this work, for me, was keeping the real killer's identity from being given away during the investigation. It was difficult to give some hints here and there while still shining the spotlight on another, as a distraction. There was a fine line here that couldn't be crossed, at least, not immediately, and it was like a balancing act to walk that line. It helped to have The Butcher intentionally raising suspicion on other suspects who could reasonably be the killer that he actually was.

Why is Kevin Harmes so obsessed? Because he believes that every wrong turn he has taken, and each incorrect assumption he has made, is being orchestrated by The Butcher, and this enrages him. As an experienced detective, the fact that a criminal like The Butcher knows that Harmes will buy his bluff and veer off in another direction is bothersome, to say the least. He almost takes this as an assault on his policing ability. Sure, people are dying, but for Harmes, that's just the tip of the iceberg. The Butcher is also basically making fun of the cops, running them around from city to city in confusion, like small children trying to catch a balloon filled with helium, but is always out of reach.

As can be expected, as the story goes on, Harmes finds little tidbits here and there which begin to clear the fog covering The Butcher's identity. Everything begins to make sense, and sure enough, the killer is someone who has been on his suspect list all along. The person has misdirected and lied to the point that it should have been obvious from the beginning. By the time Harmes is ready to nab the guy, he finds that he isn't a step ahead at all; rather, The Butcher already has a plan for this, as well, and it includes Kevin Harmes.

Box Office Butcher, with all difficulties aside, was a fun novel to write. The murder mystery genre label which it falls under afforded me much freedom; I just had to sort my way through what was believable and what would appear to be smoke and mirrors to the reader. I had to reconcile the two to each other without giving away The Butcher's identity too quickly, and hopefully, I accomplished this properly. I also had a lot of fun with The Butcher's past, though it was horrid. The abuse the guy went through at the hands of his own twisted, sick mother are enough to cause anyone to almost understand how someone could go to the kinds of extremes that this killer did.

BLOOD FEATHER AWAKENS

ISBN-13: 978-0692734087 ISBN-10: 0692734082
ISBN-13: 978-1948312189 ISBN-10: 1948312182
ISBN-13: 978-1948312172 ISBN-10: 1948312174

Crime Thriller

Of all the books I have penned, 'Blood Feather Awakens' was one of the most fun for me. It tells the story of Sam Daniels, a wildlife photographer who, while on assignment in the Amazon jungle, encounters a breathtakingly beautiful but horribly deadly, prehistoric bird. Sam witnesses the bloody killing of his guide but manages to snap a couple of grainy photographs, which he takes to an ornithologist at the University of Washington for identification. That is just the beginning of the tale; Sam and the beautiful Dr. Kate Beck, accompanied by three guides and tailed by a couple of fame-seeking paleontologists, venture back to the jungle to find, and hopefully capture, the murderous creature.

Why was this book so much fun to write? I would have to attribute it simply to the imagination involved in it. From Sam's first encounter with the bird, all the way to its capture and return to the States, I found it was a subject I could really do anything with, if I so chose. I wanted to make the time in the jungle both horrifying, thanks to the evasive bird, and romantic, due to the blossoming romance between Kate and Sam. I also wanted it to be bloody, because let's face it:

If a massive prehistoric bird were to attack, well, it would be nothing but bloody.

I also thrived on creating realistic relationships between all of the people. For instance, even though Sam and Kate are in the company of jungle guides, all of them are in this terrible situation together. It was imperative that they talk and laugh, that they come to trust and depend on each other in a way that simply would not take place on a normal jungle tour. Everyone is frightened, but they are also eager. The tour guides are also angry that one of their own has been killed, and they want the threat removed before anyone else is harmed. Sam and Kate want the bird captured and studied; they want to keep it safe while ensuring the safety of the world.

But then we have the two paleontologists, Dr. Harold Kreiger and Dr. Roy Hastings. These two men work at the University of Washington, just as Kate does. Since they are colleagues of hers, she takes Sam to see them when he brings her the photograph of the bird and recognizes it as 'prehistoric' in nature. But, just as she fears, these two begin to see how beating Kate and Sam to the punch will make them famous, and these two men try to get to the creature and locate it before Sam and Kate. This turns out bad for Kreiger and Hastings, but I have to admit, it was more than a pleasure to create the demise these two selfish men deserved.

I wanted the truth about how dangerous this thing was in my own mind to be clearly conveyed; this bird can think, reason, and use logic. The humans which pursue it may outsmart it and capture it, but all it needs is a little time to sort things out and find a way to appease its own bloodthirsty nature. This thing was never meant to be captured; after all, it survived a meteor hitting the Earth millions of years ago, and it has managed to continue its species for the sole reason that 'life will find a way'. The determination that was shown to simply survive needed to clearly reflect its ability to destroy, as well. I believe that I portrayed all of this clearly and concisely, especially at the very end.

So, what is 'Blood Feather'? To put it simply, the creature is, indeed, a bird, but it is prehistoric, related to the 'archaeopteryx' but much larger. In my mind, when humans discover the bones of prehistoric animals, all we really can do is guess as to what their real appearance would have been like. Now, perhaps they did look like that, but I venture to say that it is likely we are off a bit in our assumptions. I did nothing more than to create my own creature, in my own mind. Some of its physical traits are the same, some are different. This is the reason Kate and the paleontologists are uncertain of what it is: They are stuck with an assumed picture in their overly-educated minds.

But exactly what Blood Feather is, is not important. The bottom line is that it's a killer. It lives on flesh and blood, and it gets pleasure from the hunt and chase. It is airborne, so there really is no escape, and it has the ability to somewhat hypnotize its prey with its eerily human eyes. It is meant to confuse and terrify, which is precisely what I designed it for. Its beauty is deceptive; it will lure you in and then end your life. To be honest, this was the most fun for me: Writing about presumptuous humans who are scrambling around out of their element, trying to get the best of nature's perfect killing machine.

I truly hope readers are as entertained by this story as I was by writing it. I tried to keep it light and simple without compromising fear or blood. I also wanted to tell a story that would keep the reader turning pages. I think that those who read this fun and frightening story will appreciate it in the end, for what I intended it to be.

SHATTERED DREAMS

ISBN-10: 0997876719 ISBN-13: 978-0997876710

Crime Thriller

When I sat down to write 'Shattered Dreams', I did it with one purpose in mind, and it was a very simple purpose: To tell a story. It isn't like my other novels in that it is in no way 'supernatural' or 'psychological'; it is just the tale of a man with dreams who brought them to life, only to have them ripped away from him in the most desperate and unfair way possible. It is something that could really happen; there are no zombies or vampires, and there are no magical formulas being produced. Only a man, his dream, and the enemy who hates him.

So, let me begin with my main character, Jimmy O'Brien. Jimmy is a good boy from the beginning, the offspring of a loser Irish father and devoted Italian mother. From as far back as Jimmy can remember, he has had a single dream: To be a cop, and to fight the bad guys. He makes all the right choices, even from youth, to obtain his goal; he even goes the extra mile on more than one occasion.

Let's begin at the start, or as close to it as effectively possible. Jimmy's mother raises him alone, thanks to his father running off with another. The man had it all at one point: A wife, a son, and a good job. But rather than acting according to his priorities, he not only cheats and leaves, but he also resorts to criminal behavior that includes beating up the woman he left his wife for. Jimmy despises this behavior, even going so far as to refuse to call his father 'dad'. Along with television cop shows, it is this behavior that dictates Jimmy's hatred toward those who harm others in any criminal way.

But in his mother, Jimmy has a person who would go to the ends of the Earth for her son to be happy and well provided for. She supports him in all of his ventures, and even though she is afraid for his safety, she also backs him in his pursuit of a police career. Luciana O'Brien is a wonderful, moral woman who deserves to have something good happen to her in her life.

Jimmy has several other people who support him, from friends to the chief of his hometown police department, Matias Garcia. Over the years, all the right doors open at the right times, and Jimmy, true to his form, always walks straight through each and every one of them. Soon, he is a grown man with a job working as a real police officer, and he is nearing his goal of becoming chief for the entire department. He has a beautiful fiancé, and everything is coming together just as he had always planned.

But when an old school rival of Jimmy's comes back into the picture as a runner for the Mexican cartel, things take a terrible turn. All of his dreams are now being threatened, and before he knows it, corruption in the department is plotting to steal the dreams he has held so dear to his heart, taking everything and everyone he loves as well.

What is the point of this book? As the writer, I would have to firmly say that the point is: Nothing ever goes as planned, and more often than not, our hearts are broken terribly. Jimmy is innocent, quite literally, in this story, but by the end of the book, he is suffering consequences which only the evil should have to endure. Why? Because, to put it as simply as possible, that's life.

The things which happen to Jimmy at the hands of others are much less impactful if the reader doesn't have a firm grasp on who this young man is, morally speaking. This is someone who would rather die than do harm to another. This is someone who really couldn't tell a lie if he wanted to. Jimmy is trustworthy, soft-hearted, compassionate, and bent on doing the right thing. His every action is motivated by a solid desire to operate out of integrity, and nothing else.

All of his hardship towards the end stems from a toxic friendship he had in the first grade with a boy named Kevin Marshall. Kevin is a bad seed, through and through. When the boy gets caught for stealing from a classmate, Jimmy knows, without a doubt, that he cannot continue their friendship. But it is Kevin Marshall who Jimmy must confront in high school for dealing drugs, and it is Kevin Marshall who sparks the chain of events in adulthood which ultimately prove to be Jimmy's destruction. The point? The past will come back to haunt you, even if you weren't the one doing the haunting in the first place.

As far as Jimmy is concerned, he is a character that I have a certain amount of love for, in a literal way. I admire the man I created, and as I created his life and heartaches, I hurt for him. I found myself infuriated with the bad guys I put in his life, but at the same time, I realized I wasn't willing to bail him out of his injustices. This is the life I created for Henry James O'Brien, and this is his destiny, unfortunately.

I think readers will like this book, but not because it is frightening or abstract. Readers will enjoy it because of the level of reality they will find in its pages. I also think they will feel the same way about Jimmy that I do, and I believe they will experience anger at the unfairness that goes on in his life. In the end, 'Shattered Dreams' is a highly relatable story for anyone who decides to venture into its pages.

REQUIEM FOR THE CAGED

ISBN-10: 1948312026 ISBN-13: 978-1948312028

Romantic Suspense

Coming from the perspective of someone who creates, I believe I can say with confidence that my new book, 'Requiem for the Caged', may not be for everyone. I knew this from the start, and even as I sat down to write it, I simply wanted to tell a story I hadn't told before, and it happened to fall into a far different category than my fans are used to.

First of all, this particular story has nothing to do with the undead, or bloodsuckers of any kind. It has nothing to do with aliens, or youth potions, or tainted futuristic seas. It is a love story, pure and simple. Unconventional? Of course. But love is never really conventional in any way, now is it? So, why should it be conventional in the pages of a book?

First, I would like to begin by discussing the premise. Jason Brandtley is a good young man. He has just returned from being a prisoner of war overseas and is facing the impending death of his mother. He is a young man with a gentle spirit and full of integrity, but he has suffered many recent traumas, and with his mother being sick, they really aren't over yet. But that doesn't change the fact that his heart and soul are clean, and the motives of his heart are always based on his desire to do the right thing and help.

After his mother dies, Jason inherits the family sheep ranch, but he is having to run operations on his own. Lonely and depressed, Jason longs for a wife to share his life with. He is eager, and he is willing to do what it takes to find a good woman to walk by his side.

Andrea is a waitress who lives and works in Cheyenne, about thirty minutes away. He meets her while having lunch in the park one day, and Jason is stricken with her immediately. But Andrea is a polar opposite to Jason, as readers will see. Unlike Jason, a much-loved only child, Andrea comes from a family that is harsh and uncaring; her mother has essentially turned her back on the girl, forcing her to be strong and emotionally detached when it comes to life. The pair does have one thing in common, however: they both have suffered heartbreak several times at the hands of love interests. The thing that sets them apart is how they have chosen to respond to the pain. While Jason is able to somewhat put it behind him, Andrea's every action and reaction is based on the abuse she has suffered from men.

Jason doesn't know this, and he begins to pursue her, only to be shot down in flames and actually assaulted by her ex for his efforts. This assault sends the ex-POW over the edge, and he determines to teach Andrea a lesson. He builds a cage in his basement for her, abducts her, and refuses her release until she changes her ways.

That is as strange as this novel gets, however. It is here that the two, who are now in each other's constant company, begin to get to know one another. They begin to realize that everyone suffers heartache, but it is never a reason to re-inflict. They also begin to see each other differently in this light, and inevitably, love begins to grow.

Now, there is no torture or murder involved in this novel. The desire of Jason's heart is to genuinely help Andrea, even though he has gone to a terrifying and unacceptable length to do so. Andrea is only initially frightened of harm; she is soon convinced he couldn't hurt her if he wanted to, and this realization is the turning point in their relationship.

Why did I decide to write such a story, especially when most of my works are thrillers? Well, I would have to say that, in my opinion and from my experience, love can be the strangest and scariest thing of all. I wanted to try romantic suspense and see how two people from totally different backgrounds react to each other's pain. I wanted to play with the idea that, even if someone 'flips their lid', so to speak, they can still love and be loved. I also wanted to express the deep importance of communication in learning to love and accept one another for all that each of us is. This involves understanding that each of us is made up of all of our happiness and heartaches. Each laugh and every tear are what we consist of. Most of the time, these things can cause us to act in a manner that is repulsive or frightening, or painful, to those around us, just like in the cases of both Jason and Andrea. But these things can also be overcome if the other is willing to look at the whole person instead of just the ugly parts. That is where the beauty of love comes in.

Yes, Dear Readers, this is what you may label a 'romance' or 'love story', and that may be a jagged pill for some of you to swallow coming from me. But the fact is, love is just as much a part of life as our fear of the monster in the closet, or the stalker outside the window. It is even more a part of life than any of these because it is the basis for our sanity and survival.

It is my sincere hope that you all enjoy this book for what it is: A simple, yet complicated, tale of two people who find love in the most unlikely of places. It is the story about cages, and how all of us live in them in one way or another. Most of all, it is about acceptance of the person trapped in the cage across from yours.

OUT TO SEA

ISBN-13: 978-0997876765 ISBN-10: 099787676X
ISBN-13: 978-1948312233 ISBN-10: 1948312239
ISBN-13: 978-1948312240 ISBN-10: 1948312247

Romantic Suspense

'Out to Sea' was a project that I had to walk a fine line with. I intended for it to be a work with a very pertinent message, while forming a bond between star-crossed teen lovers that is destined to end with the cruise they were on. With the state of the future world in shambles, it was somewhat difficult to know when and where romance was truly appropriate; after all, the planet is dying before the eyes of the main characters, and they are literally watching everyone basically celebrate it. It's the sort of thing that can ruin the mood.

The basic plot of the book revolves around a chemical spill which has made all the water on Earth poisonous, even to the touch. Man has created an electrolyte-based alternative for drinking, and other methods which are less than natural are used for bathing, swimming, etc. The fact of the matter is that the end will come as a direct result of this, and most everyone is painfully aware that the future is dark and grim.

There are those, however, who have found a way to exploit the situation. The spill has made the appearance of the water indescribably gorgeous, even entrancing, to a certain level. People purchase atrociously priced luxury cruises for the sole purpose of gawking at the lifeless seas, and they seem to have no care for what the façade of beauty they are looking at really means. It is truly a horrible thing, and I wanted the level of depravity and complacency to which human beings stoop to be stark and ugly.

Tripp Young is my main character on this ocean voyage. As the only son of wealthy parents, he is expected to go on these yearly excursions with them. They are two of the countless who have bought into the horrible exploitation of the planet's impending death, and they seem blind to the reality of it all. To them, and all others like them, it is an amusement park ride, of sorts.

But Tripp is neither ignorant nor calloused to what is taking place. He looks at his existence as taking place in two categories: Before the Spill, and After the Spill, and the planets in both are very different places indeed. For a seventeen-year-old, he is very in touch with logic and sense, as well as the brokenhearted emotion he nurses for the world that was once lush with grass and other plant life; a world where you could jump in a river and swim. Tripp had to be angry, but I also knew it had to be a righteous, self-controlled anger, an anger with a purpose.

While on this joke of a cruise, Tripp meets Heidi Collins, and is instantly smitten with the smart, petite environmentally conscious redhead. Never having a real girlfriend before, he easily becomes consumed with spending as much time together while on the water as they can, and her feelings are the same. Together, they witness some pretty horrific things, which can all be attributed to the tainted sea that surrounds them. It pulls them closer and closer as the days pass.

One such scene involves a child who goes missing during the cruise. The ship's staff searches high and low for her, to no avail. Tripp, Heidi, and two of their friends watch and listen in disgusted awe as the ship continues on the water, because the show must go on. Finally, the kids decide to look for the girl themselves, on the sly.

This is one tragedy that takes place aboard the ship. It was important to convey the state of mind of those who enjoyed what the spill had done; depraved indifference and selfishness filled their souls. I contemplated the accomplishment, though it may have seemed overly dramatic in manner, at times.

As for Tripp and Heidi's love, it was doomed from the start; in my mind, this was to be a sad tale of not only the results of man's wreaking havoc on Mother Earth, but of unrequited love. These two kids genuinely love each other, and they swear to be together again. Deep inside, they both know they will not, but it is something they are not willing to even consider. I wanted the reader to feel the hopelessness and emptiness they felt at the thought of the day they would say goodbye, and I truly hope I managed to get that done. I wanted their interactions to be intensely emotional and painful, so they could be tangible to the person with the book.

To put it simply, 'Out to Sea' is an environmentally conscious romantic suspense that has no blissful ending, but it tells a story, and it teaches a lesson. It may not feel good, but lessons rarely do. I think by the end of this book, whether the reader loves it or hates it, they will never forget it. I wrote it to be the kind of story that sticks, even if it isn't popular for the particular content or level of fiction. With that being said, this is one of my personal favorites as a writer, and it had an impact on me that my other works haven't. It may be a fiction novel, but the pain and despair I put in the pages was anything but a fairy tale; I'm confident the emotion will help get the message across loud and clear.

PASSAGE OF TIME

ISBN-10: 0997876727 ISBN-13: 978-0997876727

Romantic Suspense

'Passage of Time' is actually one of my personal favorites, and I hope you enjoy reading it as much as I enjoyed writing it.

This was never intended to be a thriller novel; it just barely makes it into the science fiction realm, only doing so because of the 'fountain of youth' premise. Mostly, this book is a romantic suspense, but it is also a story of time wasted in an effort to live forever. It is a tale which has been shaped by years of regret and sadness, which are only realized at the very end.

Calvin Cooper is a man with a mission. A scientist, both by trade and by nature, Calvin wants to help others look and feel younger. Early on, he meets Elaina, the woman destined to be the love of his life and his eternal companion. Together, Calvin believes they will conquer the world. With her patience, he will come up with the end-all, be-all solution, and then they will be together forever, literally.

There is no end to Elaina's loyalty or patience. It was important to create in her, a character who is totally devoted, no matter what she may face with her man. Throughout their lives, and his work, she is his rock, and his love for her knows no bounds. Unfortunately, she is also the only one who looks at things realistically, and Calvin is destined to learn one of the most painful lessons of his life through her: People were never meant to live forever.

One situation the two endure together involves an animal rights activist group who has targeted Calvin, believing that his work involves harming animals. But even through this scary incident in their lives, Elaina is his strong tower and primary support, and his love for her grows.

Over time, Calvin begins to make progress with his formula, and while his wife is extremely supportive when it comes to meeting his goals, she is not one who believes that human beings should endure indefinitely. But she is the kind of woman who will ignore her own beliefs if it means backing up the man she loves. Calvin, however, is oblivious to all of this. The years pass, and more progress is made. As he considers all the time he has spent focusing on his work, he tries to push the guilt aside that he feels for putting poor Elaina on the back burner. He reassures himself that when the formula is perfected, the two of them will enjoy eternity in each other's arms.

Ralph Gordon is another character who was necessary to the lesson Calvin is set to learn. Ralph comes on as Calvin's assistant, and they too end up forging an unbreakable friendship. He, like Elaina, is dedicated, and he truly cares about the person who is doing all the work. But Ralph just wants to live his days out in peace; living forever isn't even remotely attractive to him. Calvin seems to be stuck in a huge lack of understanding; both Ralph and Elaina could spell things out for him, but his genius has stolen his ability to look at things from the heart. Without Ralph, Calvin would likely just consider that Elaina's opinions are formed because she is something of an emotional woman.

Another character who tries to get the point across, in a much more subdued manner, is Noah Carter, the sick old man who first owned Maddie, the horse. But when given the option to continue on, permanently, in his newfound youth, Noah gratefully refuses, explaining his stance clearly and concisely. This is yet another example of Calvin being so blinded by his dreams that he has become numb to life's realities; he has no grasp whatsoever on why these people would refuse, nor is he able to consider giving up.

Calvin Cooper is, in a sense, every man. Anyone with any level of personal accountability or love in their heart wants to give the world to those who are the objects of his affection. If that man is able to cause his wife to live forever, he would, as would Calvin. But Calvin has lost touch with the very things that make us all human, and in his effort to work literal miracles, he allows his entire life to pass him by. It isn't until he comes to the point of being surrounded in his success while in utter isolation that Calvin begins to understand what he gave up for a dream that was never meant to become a reality.

Yes, I wrote 'Passage of Time' to be a love story. I wrote it with the intent of making readers feel the love between Calvin and Elaina in a very tangible sense, and I hope I succeeded in that goal. But above and beyond that, this book was meant to make the reader consider who they have to love, and whether or not they are doing all that they can to demonstrate that love during the limited time they have. As we all know, there is no secret potion, no 'ElainaYouth' to consume that will give us countless years to revel in the gift of life. What each of us has, all that we have, is the here and now that ultimately makes up that thing we call 'today'.

So, in consideration of the above, I believe that mature readers will find 'Passage of Time' to be compelling and thought-provoking. I believe it will stimulate a spirit of gratefulness, when allowed, and I also believe it will leave readers with the simple satisfaction of having read a good book. In the end, that is the purpose of fiction, after all, and 'Passage of Time' is no exception.

DEAD ON THE WATER

ISBN-10: 0997876700 ISBN-13: 978-0997876703
ISBN-10: 1948312905 ISBN-13: 978-1948312905
ISBN-10: 1948312921 ISBN-13: 978-1948312929
ISBN-10: 194831293X ISBN-13: 978-1948312936

Zombie Thriller

This is another zombie contribution which I put a bit of a spin on. 'Dead on the Water' chronicles the story of a Fantasy Lines cruise ship which has a passenger who got bit by a dog during a shopping spree with her parents in Belize. Not knowing that the dog is carrying a terrible, zombie-making virus, the bite-victim re-boards the ship, and it returns to the vast ocean. Soon, the entire vessel is overrun with zombies, and those who have not been infected are fighting for their lives in the middle of the sea.

The first thing I would like to say about this particular book is that I allowed the zombies to be able to think, speak, and function, but they are the undead, nevertheless. The leader of the zombie pack, Captain James McElroy, even continues to be the leader in death that he was in life, and his plan is to not only take over the entire ship, but to get to land and carry on spreading the vile sickness when they dock in Houston.

This is a fast-paced book; once the action starts, it is pretty much non-stop. Being on a cruise ship, those who are still normal have very limited resources or means of escape. The ship has approximately three-thousand zombies trying to get to the last remaining survivors, so most of the ship's staff that are still alive are essentially barricaded into one part of the ship or another, including the bridge and a fitness center. They are desperate, with no weapons and no way to get off the ship without guaranteeing their own demise.

While it is about zombies, and there are several very graphic scenes, I do not believe it is necessarily a scary book. I tried to use dialogue in a surreal manner, especially coming from the monsters, in an effort to show the craziness and terrifying truth about the situation, but I didn't want it to be too heavy. My vision was simply to relate the hopelessness of the situation without making the book burdensome to read; I wanted it to be on the 'lighter' side, if possible.

Now, I presented a couple of different situations in the book. The primary one takes place on the ship; the second is happening at a shady lab in Belize, where the girl was bitten by a dog in the alley. This lab is sort of an underground operation run by a somewhat 'mad' scientist and his assistant, Bruce Ward; the good doctor relocated after the States stopped his experimentation. The long and short of it is that this lab has gone haywire, and its infected rats are beginning to run rampant. The CDC tries to gain control of this situation, which is sort of a side-line story to give you, the reader, a bit of hope that this craziness will be contained. I should warn you, especially my new readers: Don't get your hopes up. I find it difficult to imagine happy endings when it comes to the genres I write in, and I find it much easier to be horribly realistic. But let's face it, I write about completely unrealistic stuff. What I'm trying to say is, the glory of fiction is in its falseness, but the impact of fiction is found in its painful reality. If a zombie apocalypse really happened, would the ending really be a good one? I think not; it would be hopeless and desperate, and that is the painful reality of this book.

Speaking of hope, let's talk about George Meade, Captain McElroy's assistant. So, we have the CDC battling things on land, but those still living on the ship are literally fighting a losing battle; they are fish in a barrel. If the zombies reach land, there will be a literal outbreak, and nothing the CDC is doing in Belize will matter. I allow George to escape in a lifeboat because someone on that damn cruise ship has to be smart enough to get away and get help. Pretty daunting task, don't you think? To reach the docking point before the ship, baking in the sun with no water, and having been through a terribly traumatic and unbelievable experience? Well, all I have to say about his success or failure is, you'll just have to see.

On another topic, I didn't get too deep with any of the characters as far as their personal appearance or personalities. There are many characters in 'Dead on the Water'; only a few hold the limelight, and none for very long; ultimately, it is 'every man for himself'.

So, as far as my second zombie tale goes, I hope you enjoy it. It's a little lighter than you might expect, but it is fast-paced, and you'll find plenty of gruesome scenes. 'Dead on the Water' is an easy and entertaining read. I hope you'll check out this book, and have fun reading it, too!

PERMANENT INK

ISBN-10: 0997876735 ISBN-13: 978-0997876734

Zombie Thriller

I wrote 'Permanent Ink' with mostly one message to convey: The price of greed can be astronomical, and most often, it is horribly destructive.

This is the story of a stationers' company that is on the brink of bankruptcy, but they have an ace in the hole: A new ink that appears almost holographic once it is on paper. Knowing that the kids will love it, Aspen Stationers' pushes for quick release of the pens developed to dispense the ink, wanting it available for public purchase before the school year starts. But the executives at Aspen have a secret: In the lab, the ink has had an adverse effect on rats, causing them to attack each other to the death, then bringing them back to life more violent and bloodthirsty than ever. Because this only happens when the ink is still wet, Aspen has convinced themselves that the world will be safe, and consumers will be none the wiser.

In an effort to show how widespread the destruction is, I scattered the storyline around a bit: One particular incident involving the ink takes place in a hospital in Thornton, Colorado. Another, in Aspen, where the company is located, and finally Monte Vista. The outbreak is taking place in the suburbs, but the local government is trying to figure things out, and has even called in the CDC. The catastrophe has even reached other areas, but for the sake of the story, I have kept the text limited to areas in Colorado.

First, let's look at the outbreak at the hospital. When a young girl gets the ink in a scrape, she is soon terribly ill. Her mother rushes her to the hospital to be seen, and the child is admitted. Even though she is exhibiting strange, and even violent, behavior, her mother is driven to comfort her, which leads to an attack. Before anyone even understands what is taking place, the 'zombie' sickness has spread like wildfire, and both patients and employees of the health care center are forced to fight for their lives. A pair of physicians are beginning to figure things out, slowly but surely, but will they solve the problem before it's too late?

The hospital scenes are fast-paced; it is chaos there, and the panic the characters are feeling should be tangible. I did the best I could to convey this, without giving too much hope to the situation, because frankly, I felt the situation in Thornton was fairly close to being hopeless.

In the situation with Aspen Stationers' scientist, Randy Carstens, he is fully aware of the potential for disaster, and he is sickened by the complacency of the executives in charge. Randy manages to get himself fired, but that doesn't keep him from returning and trying to stop the ball, which has already been set rolling. While there, the company's CEO, Roger McGinley, falls victim to the zombie rats while trying to force Randy to comply at gunpoint. Fortunately,

Randy is able to escape and notify Aspen Police, but by the time they understand what is happening, they have a pretty big mess on their hands.

Which takes us to Brian Olson, a soon-to-be ninth grader at Monte Vista High School. Brian's single mother couldn't afford to buy him the expensive pen, but his best friend Caleb comes through. Brian tests the ink, which is said to smudge easily, with a finger. Unfortunately, he has a papercut, and the ink gets into his bloodstream. Overnight, the boy has died and becomes one of the bloodthirsty undead; his poor, unsuspecting mother is his first victim. Soon, the town is pretty much on lockdown, and the petrified people of Monte Vista are waiting for the CDC to come and save the day.

'Permanent Ink' is a zombie story, plain and simple, filled with the flesh-eating monsters that are all the rage at the current time. It is meant to gross readers out, to a certain extent, but mostly, with all of the chaotic scenes aside, I wanted to really convey a message. Corporate greed is the catalyst behind this horrible outbreak, wreaking havoc on unsuspecting consumers who have been blindsided by their timely marketing tactics. The worst part is, Aspen Stationers' is more than suspicious of the potential for damage that the ink has; they know full well what it can do, and they just don't care. This type of manipulation takes place every day in our world, with results just as destructive, only slower and less obvious. This truth is really what is behind the message in this book.

Of course, things have to be cleared up, and solutions must be found so life can go on. But as I mentioned earlier, I neither saw nor felt any positive resolution to this particular story, and as a writer, I had to struggle to make a way for the sun to rise on these towns again, with hope. I firmly believe that, if this were a true story, there would be no one left to write about it; the world would be taken out systematically by the undead, which Aspen Stationers' created when they released Lumiosa ink to the public.

It is my hope that readers are able to enjoy this book for what it truly is: A work of fiction that provides yet another take on zombies and how they might come to be walking, and terrorizing, among us. It is meant for entertainment, but I think the moral behind this made-up tale makes it possible to consider other possibilities, and hopefully, it causes readers to think about the items they are willingly choosing to consume.

LIVING LEGACY

ISBN-13: 978-0692517246 ISBN-10: 0692517243
ISBN-13: 978-1948312196 ISBN-10: 1948312190
ISBN-13: 978-1948312202 ISBN-10: 1948312204

Zombie Thriller

'Living Legacy: Among the Dead' is the first complete book I wrote. Though it is a very quick read, I believe readers will get just as much out of its pages as they would if it were a larger novel. Mostly, it was written for the sake of the love story which I have woven into the apocalyptic situation.

Alicia Gaden is a biology major at UCLA; she has her goals lined up and her future planned. She is also a very good student and person; she doesn't galivant around with different boys or party. Rather, she remains single, and keeps her primary focus on her studies.

Jace Booth is pretty much the same type of person as Alicia, with the exception being that he majors in chemistry. The pair meet up when everyone starts changing; people become violent, and their skin begins to pale and rot. For some reason, the two of them seem to have avoided drinking the water, allowing them to survive the strange phenomenon taking place, but together they pursue knowledge regarding why this is happening. As it turns out, there are no two better for the job.

The book is told from Alicia's perspective, which is not typical for me. I wanted to convey the zombie outbreak from the female point of view.

Alicia, in the initial pages, is pretty much on her own. Sure, she has a roommate, Lilith, but the girl really doesn't have much of a purpose, except for the sake of the reality of college life. No, Alicia is witnessing the changes in others entirely on her own. She wants to figure out what is happening and why it doesn't seem to be happening to her. She meets Jace during a trip to the UCLA student library, which turns out to be a relief because he seems unaffected as well.

Unbeknownst to the two of them, the problem is in the LA water supply. All-Purpose Plastics has been developing the 'plastic of the future': Soligel. Unfortunately, they push it through for federal approval, and an unaware maintenance man ends up disposing of a chemical spill improperly. He, too, is affected, but corporate executives take matters into their own hands and shut him up for good. It is only through their own tests and dangerous missions that Alicia and Jace are able to figure out that the problem is in the water. Once that is pinpointed, they must come up with a way to solve the outbreak before it is too late.

I wanted the main characters to be highly intelligent, but I also wanted them to be as courageous as possible. Let's face it, and I am sad to say, most college students today would panic and buckle if they found themselves in this situation. If these two are going to survive, and if any love is going to grow between them, it was essential for them to be strong and determined, and to have a mutually beneficial skill set if they wanted to get the job done. These are the main characteristics that were the foundation for Jace Booth and Alicia Gaden.

Now, it is true that I didn't really deal with the executives of All-Purpose Plastics in a manner that would be satisfying. The fact is, to me, they would be succumbing to the outbreak in their own time and manner. In order for the book to have the combined flavors that I gave it, there was no room for justice, at least, not the kind of justice these people rightfully deserved. Greed and malice are sicknesses of the soul; it was best to let karma deal with them and focus on Alicia and Jace.

I added the tidbit regarding Alicia possibly becoming pregnant for a couple of different reasons. First, it would solidify their relationship and drive them on to continue the fight at hand at any cost. I wanted the relationship between the two of them to be held together by more than sex; my intent with these two was a lifelong commitment, even if there was the possibility that life could end at any second. Second, a pregnancy would be representative of life finding a way; this gives the reader a renewed sense of hope, both for the lives of the main characters, and for their success in completing their mission against the zombies and the tainted water.

I also wanted them to be able to conduct their research in a setting that provided them with some level of peace and comfort. This is where the house comes in. It was owned by a zombie victim named Belinda Smythe, who is caught off guard by the undead monsters. Her car is left there, and has run itself out of gasoline. Finding this location was essential to their success; I mean, let's be real: If a couple of college kids are going to save the day and fall in love while they're at it, having a comfortable base of operations is essential.

Without giving away the ending, I would just like to say that Alicia and Jace are very crafty, and they have more than enough reasons to accomplish their goal to defeat the zombies and fix the issue successfully. But as we all know, a good story never ends without some kind of lure or suggestion about the real state of things. Perhaps Alicia and Jace firmly believe that they have fixed the problem in the water, but did they really? Only time will tell. I sincerely hope that readers enjoy 'Living Legacy: Among the Dead', and appreciate it for the fun piece of fiction it was meant to be.

ZOMBIE DIARIES

Homecoming Junior Year
ISBN-10: 0997876778 ISBN-13: 978-0997876772
Winter Formal Junior Year
ISBN-10: 0997876786 ISBN-13: 978-0997876789
Prom Junior Year
ISBN-10: 0997876794 ISBN-13: 978-0997876796

Girl Zombie

'Zombie Diaries" is a series I have written about the funny, off-beat story of Mavis Harvey, Girl Zombie. In the beginning of this first installment, the main character inadvertently drinks tainted tap water, and as the book progresses, she begins to experience some fairly crazy changes. As the introductory novel to the series, readers will get to know Mavis a bit, and they will get a strong sense of the personality of this girl who is slowly turning into a flesh-eating monster.

This is not a horror novel in the traditional sense, and I never intended it to be. What I wanted to do with Mavis and her life was have fun by asking, 'What would it be like if a normal, everyday girl were to experience this type of change alone, out of the blue? What if she retained her intelligence and logic, realizing something was happening, but not sure what? How would she deal with it?' I wanted the book to be light, with a tad of humor, and I wanted it to contain a story that was acceptable for reading for an audience of most any age.

In the beginning stages of Mavis' journey, she feels a little off but soon finds that her appetite has grown out of control overnight. She is a slight girl, so this gets the attention of her mother, who believes she is ill and takes Mavis to the doctor. Insisting that she feels great, and with no other real symptoms other than insatiable hunger, her physician diagnoses her with anemia, directs her to take iron supplements, and tells her mother to let her eat when she wants for the time being.

Unbeknownst to those in her life, Mavis soon begins to crave more than just an overabundance of food; she wants raw meat, and the bloodier the better. I used raw liver (of any kind) as her 'snack', so to speak, for a couple of different reasons. One: There really isn't a bloodier meat with a grosser texture; it seems to fit as a zombie snack perfectly, and two: Because most everyone hates liver, and the thought of it raw is unbearable. The temptation to gross out my readers was as irresistible to me as raw liver is to Mavis.

As her 'illness' slowly progresses, it begins to come out a bit in gray flaky spots on her skin and prominent dark veins showing through her flesh. She is getting pale, and her mother worries about that fact. Mavis also gains no weight, which is strange, because she is constantly eating one thing or another. Jane Harvey only mentions her concerns in passing, but when she catches her daughter eating a raw pork chop bone, she feels justified in her concerns. Mavis is a loving daughter and has always been trustworthy. Because she feels fine, she is able to tell her mother to not be worried, 'It's just the anemia'; Jane believes her.

I also felt that it was important to make Mavis very likeable; I wanted her to have strong morals and goals. She is very friendly and kindhearted, but she doesn't hang around with a lot of friends. Indeed, she has only one, Kim Coleman, and they have been best friends since the first grade.

She likes boys, but has never been on a date simply because school has been more important, but also because she has never been asked. While she is pretty and slender, she also seemed a bit bookish and nerdy to the opposite sex; she knows it, and it never bothered her before. Kim is a bit heavy, very pretty, and just a tad self-absorbed; she has never dated either, possibly because of her friendship with Mavis.

After Mavis is 'infected', she is asked on her first date ever. A star football player for her high school tells her he has liked her for a long time, and works up the courage to ask her to the homecoming dance. At this point readers may begin to see Mavis as the teenager she is; as she begins to get to know love interest Jeff Deason, her feminine side begins to really show through her words and actions.

Mavis likes him very much, and she is excited about going to the dance with someone other than her best friend. The problem begins, however, when the pair start to date before the big event. She realizes that she can smell him, and he smells delicious, but so do a lot of other people.

With no real worries, she continues to get to know the young man and live her life, but when she dreams of eating a delivery man one day, she vows to never do such a horrible act. She is shocked and dismayed at her own dreams, but not because she killed a man; she is ashamed because she ate him, and that is the only reason. Convinced it is best to keep the dream to herself, Mavis continues with her plans for homecoming night with Jeff.

I didn't intend for ZD1 to be bloody, or scary. What my vision for Mavis consisted of was something laid-back and fun to read, something that takes an already insane idea (zombies) and turns it into a story that takes away the sting of the same old idea. With that in mind, readers of any age will enjoy the story of Mavis, and they will want to stick this crazy experience out with her until the bitter end.

I encourage you to enjoy 'Zombie Diaries' and continue to follow this tongue-in-cheek heroine as she slowly, but surely, comes to terms with what is happening to her.

OVERTAKEN CAPTIVE STATES

ISBN-13: 978-1948312004 ISBN-10: 194831200X
ISBN-13: 978-0692489314 ISBN-10: 0692489312
ISBN-13: 978-1948312127 ISBN-10: 1948312123

Supernatural Thriller

This particular novel was the second book that I have written, and it is the only one I have penned with a focus on alien invasion. I think that the premise of the book is good, and the story is fairly spooky overall.

The prologue consists of nothing but random characters in scattered cities. It relates the very first moments of the invasion of the Oppressors from varying points of view. As far as an introduction goes, it is superficial, but it is effective because of this fact. Once the invasion becomes confirmed reality, I introduce the main characters of the book and tell the story.

This is an invasion story that really doesn't have the obligatory 'happy ending'; nothing about this situation could possibly end happily for humans, and I wasn't going to pretend it could. But to me, the invasion itself is not the scariest part of 'Overtaken'; being tested to determine if you are of enough value to live or die is even more frightening. The pressure of the situation, and the truth that even if you pass the tests, you will go to a foreign planet forever, is a grim thing to have on one's shoulders. In the real world, people would commit suicide if faced with the prospect.

But there always has to be a hero or two, even if they ultimately are only saving themselves. The character of Josh Nichols takes readers to Washington, DC, with front row seats. Josh works as a code writer at the Pentagon. He is a young, ambitious man with all of his supposed ducks in a row. Something of a workaholic, Josh has no family or girlfriend in DC; he was born and raised in Iowa, so he's still fairly green behind the ears.

Kamryn Reynolds is Josh's polar opposite. With a history of crime and street-life, she is a seasoned, semi-tough computer hacker who is always dodging the law. When the invasion takes place, these two meet accidentally, and soon Josh is working side-by-side with her for the president himself. Together, they search for a weak spot in the computer system that is running all of the alien spacecrafts. Their plan is to hack into it and let down protective shields, making the Oppressors open to human attack.

In an effort to pick up the pace, I gave humankind a deadline, so to speak. In large numbers, people are led to testing facilities, separated from their families and never to be seen again. These groups are done by sections throughout each included city. Josh and Kamryn must get this all figured out before they are herded away for themselves.

What is the testing for? This was the fun part for me, because the concept does spark fear in my heart. So, am I being tested for strengths, or weaknesses?

What will be done to me, extermination-wise, if I fail either way? Worse yet, what will happen to me if I 'pass'? It all consists of question marks which dance gleefully around the unknown, and the unknown is the scariest thing in the world.

Now, we should probably consider the question: With all of the resources and skills at the fingertips of the United States government, especially when it comes to employees, why choose Josh and Kamryn to try and save the day? Well, dear reader, I think the answer is obvious: It makes for a story that is much more fun and relatable. But seriously, isn't it hard to relate to every super-hero character there is? Real life consists of real people, and that's what these two kids represent.

'Superior' is another character I enjoyed playing with. He is the soulless, alien leader of the Oppressors, and his mission is destruction to his gain. He couldn't care less about these 'humans'. To him, they are like cockroaches in a deserted house; they must be exterminated before the new tenants can move in. From that perspective, it is his nature to be who he is and do what he is doing to humanity, just as it is our nature to love puppies and kitties and show compassion. The Oppressors are not able to think or feel in the same way.

The president, and all of his high-end, star-spangled advisors, are at a loss. The reason for this is simple: If aliens came, and they had the technology to get here, chances are they have it over on us. It would be a

losing battle if indeed we had to fight one. None of
their computer geniuses think like Kamryn or Josh,
which forces the president's hand. I almost wrote these
high-rankers as 'bumbling', because that's how I saw
them in my mind's eye. They have been so busy
thinking they were omnipotent that they never stopped
to think about their own mortality. Bumbling, like I
said.

Then we have the end. Yes, there are survivors; the
Oppressors promised there would be. But there are
more victims than escapees; the planet is virtually
demolished. Not to mention the people who didn't
pass and were killed, or worse yet, the ones stranded on
the blazing, crumbling planet. I feel safe when I say
there are no winners here, but there wouldn't be if this
ever really happened, either.

I liked the way all of the 'hows' and 'whys' worked
out the way they did. I hope readers have a good time
with this grim story, and I hope that they get out of it
all I put into it: From the fiction to the fear.

LUCIFER'S ANGEL

ISBN-13: 978-0692733288 ISBN-10: 0692733280
ISBN-13: 978-1948312219 ISBN-10: 1948312212
ISBN-13: 978-1948312226 ISBN-10: 1948312220

Supernatural Thriller

'Lucifer's Angel' is a book which tells the tale of a young girl raised in a very religious home, who experiences a year of terrible loss. The result of these painful occurrences is loss of the faith she has had her entire life, and in an effort to find a 'god' she can trust, the young teen turns to witchcraft. Unfortunately, she has no idea what she is getting herself into, and the consequences of her choice to revert are devastating.

Sarah Hathaway is your average teenager. She has lived in the fictional town of Paradise, her entire life, the only child of her parents, and their pride and joy. She has a very normal, happy life: Sarah has her best friend, Michelle, and her beloved border collie, Mitzi. She also has an uncommonly close relationship with her grandmother, church pianist Emma Holt. Everything in her life is perfect, and she is completely unprepared for the series of tragedies that take place.

For me, the best thing about writing 'Lucifer's Angel' was the freedom I had to add as many twists and surprises as I saw fit. This is an unpredictable book, and I like it that way. Even to the very last pages, when you finally think you have what is happening to Sarah figured out, I switch it up. But what I have to say is that the nature of this book is the perfect breeding ground for such surprise, and without it, this would not have come anywhere near making the point I intended it to make.

So, then, what is the point? Well, I could say there are a few, in fact. First, it is safe to say that we should never dabble in something we know nothing about. Hidden dangers lurk around every last corner in this world, and matters of spirituality are no exception. Whether you are a religious person or not, this is a fact, and Sarah learns this in a terrifying and painful way. Unfortunately for her, this lesson comes late.

Secondly, pain is a part of life. All of us go through doubt about our own beliefs and abilities. Sarah's doubt happens to run so deep, and her heart is so broken, that she makes the choice to turn to witchcraft almost strictly out of a sense of revenge toward God. 'If you won't give me my way, I'll find someone who will,' is essentially her thought process. Of course she is hurting, but we all do, and no one is exempt. When we turn our back on our own knowledge and beliefs because we are pouting over the facts of life, we sort of get what we deserve in the end. No amount of revenge or fit throwing will change the fact that bad things happen every single day.

I also try to convey the fact that it is terribly dangerous to give others too much trust. There are those in life that hold positions that should be trustworthy... pastors, parents, teachers, and the like. But we all know too well that everyone is human, and human beings are selfish by nature, not to mention capable of horrible things, no matter what their title or position is. This is especially true if there is something valuable to gain.

First, poor Sarah's grandmother passes while they are together. They are close, and this is the first death the girl ever experiences. She is torn apart, but after a bit, she tries to find her footing in life once again. Right after that, her dog is violently killed; since she is just getting over Grandma, this is like ripping a scab off a wound. Now it is a little harder for her to find her way back into the light. Suddenly, her lifelong best friend is moving two-thousand miles away... another great loss. The final straw is, her mother dies of cancer; all of these things happen in a very short period of time.

Besides her father, the only people she has for support are those from the church, and they are the last people she wants to talk to. Sarah begins to dabble in the craft, just studying and dabbling. After being bullied at school, resulting in personal injury, she decides to cast a spell on the culprit, and much to her great pleasure, it works. Next, she and new boyfriend Ryan Morris cast another, this time for money; this is just to confirm the power at their fingertips.

But things begin to take a scary turn. Ryan gets sick, and Sarah discovers someone evil is controlling the events in Sarah's life from the shadows, and the reason they are doing this is more devious and terrible than anyone can imagine. It takes the help of church member Laura McCain to educate Sarah and help her to confront the darkness which is threatening to consume her.

Yes, once again I have added surprises. Yes, I have twisted things in all the right places. But as I said above, this type of thing would be the nature of the black arts anyway; don't be surprised. The only thing I will admit to here is that I wish things could have gone differently for Sarah in her life; she is a likeable young lady who has promise. Unfortunately, her anger and decisions are her own worst enemy, and ultimately and sadly, this plays out in her life for you to read.

I hope you enjoy reading 'Lucifer's Angel', both for the joy of reading and for the points I have tried to make. It is a creative effort that consists of grief, horror, a bit of romance, and desperation. I have written about witchcraft before, but this story should drive things home and make them a bit more real.

STOLEN BLOOD

ISBN-10: 0997876743 ISBN-13: 978-0997876741

Vampire Thriller

'Stolen Blood' is the story of a secret society of vampires, all of whom live and work among us amicably, without murder or the intent to commit it. The difference between 'Stolen Blood' and other 'functional' vampire works which I have written is that these vampires are able to live the way they do through a pact with the 'Dark Father', to whom they offer a regular sacrifice in return for the ability to live off donated blood.

While I created several vampires who actively participate in this tale, the two main bloodsuckers are Mason Stout and Ira Stone. Mason has worked his way up to be the mayor of Philadelphia, Pennsylvania, while Ira Stone is the head of the massive conglomeration Stone and Kimble Pharmaceuticals. Stone also is the head of the secret society, and along with his wise assistant, is the only one permitted to seek out the will of the Dark Father in any given situation.

This society obtains their blood from a middleman by the name of Ross Berry. Berry is a gambling addict, something of a low-life, but he has the connections needed to obtain donated blood from a company called Bio-Donor, which he, in turn, sells at an atrocious price to the Society. But something happens along the line to Ross, disrupting this 'perfect' arrangement, and motivating Mayor Stout to seek out the assistance of another, Ross's friend and sidekick, Mike Biela. This is when the trouble begins.

The blood obtained by Mike is essentially 'bad', having undergone testing and other unknown 'treatment', which consists of genetic mutation. It is intended for the treatment of cancer, but Mike and those in the Society are unaware of this. Now, Mason Stout and those in his society 'sector' have consumed this blood, and it has reverted them back to the murderous state which they originally possessed. In a blood-induced 'high', Stout kills Mike Biela, and has to find the source of blood for himself, which he does, but only after killing a security guard and single father. Now, Stout must face the guard's grief-stricken and enraged daughter Sasha Hunter, who is being protected under the watchful eyes of Ira Stone; the leader knows that Stout must be stopped if the Society is to have any chance for redemption in the eyes of the Dark Father.

The first point I would like to make, which is vital to the story, is that while Mason Stout is the mayor of a major US city, he is also an egotist whose arrogant condition is aggravated by the bad blood. Sure, he is part of the Society, and he is being cared for by the Dark Father regardless of the negative state of his heart, but when his amplified condition puts all at risk, it is nothing to have to rid the earth of him.

Ira Stone is also a vampire, but his heart is in a much healthier state from the beginning. As the leader of the Society, it is his responsibility to make sure the others are cared for. Mason Stout manages to lose many who reside in his sector, and this fact alone is enough to make him a liability that needs to go. So, why is the help of the lamenting Sasha Hunter enlisted? Because she is obsessed as well as angry and because Ira is not able to do the deed himself; the elimination of Stout must be done by an outsider. Vigilante justice is the perfect solution.

Now, let's talk about the relationship between Ira and Sasha. Ira quickly gains her trust, almost stepping into the shoes of her deceased father immediately. Though she has no idea that the man is a vampire, she recognizes that he has the same intention as she: To rid the world of the murderous beast that killed her dad, though they both want this for differing reasons. Ira and Sasha quickly become fond of each other, and it takes little to no effort for her to trust this strange older man completely.

'Stolen Blood' is something of a far-fetched story that is heavy with originality and creativity. While it is a story about vampires, it is even more so a story about good versus evil, regardless of the fact that Ira Stone is at the helm when it comes to Mason's demise. It is important to understand that the Society, while made up of vampires, has crossed over into a new existence because of the Dark Father, which has pretty much rendered them 'good guys'.

As a heroine, Sasha Hunter is motivated by rage and deep grief. Anyone could have approached her with the killing of Stout and she would have jumped on the chance. To me, though, it was vital that the 'father figure' type do this, and as the compassionate and sensible leader of the Society, Stone was the ideal candidate to approach her, educate her, and train her, even though he had ulterior motives she has no idea about.

When I wrote this novel, I wanted to put a new skew on the whole vampire idea. This is not the first time I have done this, as long-time fans well know. Anyone familiar with my DeSai Trilogy is already aware that I enjoy creating vampires who live and walk among us, and 'Stolen Blood' is another of that sort.

This is a fun novel which definitely has its horrible moments. The concept is off-beat, but most readers enjoy a change as much as I revel in writing about one.

IN THE DEPTHS

(DeSai Trilogy Book 1)
ISBN-10: 0692721932 ISBN-13: 978-0692721933

Supernatural Thriller

This was the first installment of a vampire trilogy that I wrote involving a witch who is seeking immortality and all power by seducing the omnipotent head vampire of all time. It was also the first vampire book I wrote, and to be honest, one of the most detailed and fun books I have written. I believe that this ongoing saga is deep, engaging, and entertaining.

Cyril DeSai is a centuries-old vampire who has been wreaking havoc and causing terror in the hearts of men the world over. There is more to his behavior than simply murderous feeding; Cyril wants a family of his own that he can lord over and 'love'. In order for that to properly happen, he needs a queen, and finding the right woman is at the heart of his quest. Unfortunately, not just anyone will do; most women give in to his every desire, and he needs one who is capable of taking care of the 'family' in his unforeseen absence, one who will keep his dream alive.

'In the Depths' is written in a manner which allows the fictional vampire characters to live and walk among us. Once DeSai gets the ball rolling by attacking a SCUBA diver in the depths of a cave in Honduras, it is just a matter of time before his kind slowly begins to take over, and this will bring him to full power, in accordance with his plan. The Earth, ultimately, will belong to him, and it will exist only under his rule or the rule of his queen, once she is found. I enjoyed toying with this idea; the thought of all of us wandering around, living our day to day lives without suspicion is basically what we all do every day. Having vampires run the show is pretty much representative of the governments that rule over us. This is one thing that differs in this vampire story when it is compared to others.

Another point that differs and takes this story on its own unique path is the concept of a witch 'mating' with a vampire, and even being bitten for the sole purpose of enjoying life eternal. She is already evil to the core, with her own selfish motives lying at the root of every decision she makes. The outcome, while initially unknown, is the basis for the other two installments in this trilogy, and there are some interesting ideas I added here and there in regards to what would happen if such a union were to take place, even in the fictional realm.

So, with Cyril DeSai seeking all power, Rasia Engres enters the picture. Rasia comes from a long line of witches, and while most of them were 'good' witches (or at least, behaved in a socially acceptable manner), Rasia is rotten through and through. She has basically hated men and their incessant sexual advances for her entire life, so seeking out a true vampire and usurping his plans means nothing to her.

Rasia is strikingly beautiful, with long, lush red hair and emerald eyes. She is slender and toned, and extremely confident in all of her ways. Now, DeSai has always been able to have any woman he wants; he is extremely attractive himself, and his hypnotic manner and ability turn each of them into putty in his hands. Typically, he tires of them quickly, but Rasia is a different story. The beautiful journalist sweeps him off his feet with little effort, and it doesn't take long for the bird to become the prey.

While DeSai is nothing more than a black-hearted spawn of Satan, I wanted him to be somewhat likeable for the reader. I wanted him to be loaded with such sex appeal and confidence that even his most morbid behaviors became easy to overlook. In the first pages, this was a bit difficult, because realistically, Cyril DeSai is a murderous vampire. But once Rasia comes onto the scene, this daunting task lightened a bit. The 'victor' is to become the victim; now the reader is able to sympathize with him on a different level, which honestly sets the tone for both of the next two books.

Is this trilogy far-fetched? Of course! It's a vampire witch story! But it is highly enjoyable directly due to its unbelievability. The point here is not 'Could this really happen'. The point is: what would happen if a witch was able to secure a vampire bite successfully? And what if she was a bad witch by nature? And worse yet, what if she became the head of the most powerful country in the world?

It is also important to point out that, while the people of Earth are all being changed into vampires, those who haven't yet been changed have no idea about the monsters they are surrounded by, and this is part of the big plan. It is an easy takeover for DeSai, a takeover which is based almost slowly on his ability to sweet talk, manipulate and lie. So, is his destiny with Rasia deserved? Almost absolutely! Even after readers learn who he was in the past, before his 'fall' to evil, after they learn of his children and wife, and the way he became who he is, it is impossible to ignore the fact that he is now, a killer. Sympathy may go out the window, but I intended to recreate any feelings of pity one may have for DeSai when I wrote the two follow-up books; I believe I accomplished that goal, as readers will discover when they continue with two and three.

I was highly entertained with the smug, selfish nature of the characters, and it was a joy to bring them to life as I did. I only hope readers enjoy them as much as I did writing them.

WITCHES IMMORTAL

(DeSai Trilogy Book 2)
ISBN-10: 0692722165 ISBN-13: 978-0692722169

Supernatural Thriller

'Witches Immortal' is the second installment in my DeSai Trilogy. Essentially, this series is a vampire tale, but in this, book two, the main character, Rasia Engres, is also a witch. The entire point, besides being an entertaining work of fiction, is to find out about the woman who killed DeSai in book one on a much more personal level.

Rasia is a witch through and through, and she really doesn't have an ounce of love in her soul. This is something I wanted to make clear in 'In the Depths', but even more so here. The most effective way to do that, in my opinion, was to let the readers really get to know her and have an understanding of the reality that a number of circumstances made her who she is. Excuses aside, the woman is evil to the core, and she is truly the perfect mother for the child she is carrying.

So, as readers get to know Rasia, they will also get the scoop on Cyril DeSai from a differing perspective of that given in the first book. Now things are all about the woman who took his life: how she came to know who and what he was, and how she pretty much put herself in a position to take things over. She is crafty and conniving, and she won't think twice about causing pain to another for whatever reason.

Rasia Engres is also a very beautiful woman; her high intelligence level is simply the icing on the cake. She is a tall, slender woman with red hair and green eyes, and her taste in clothing is impeccable. Being a professional woman who is actively climbing the ladder of success, she is able to impose her stern personality often, especially with co-workers and underlings.

Intimate relationships don't really interest her; in fact, she was a virgin when she gave herself to DeSai. Rasia has other things on her mind in life, and they have nothing to do with lying around and making love. She has also been put in very uncomfortable positions by men in her life, as you will read, and this had stirred up a fair amount of rage toward the opposite sex. This point contributes greatly to her virginity being intact for so long in her life.

Rasia can be driven to do 'good', if I could call it that, but only if there is something in it for her. Take, for instance, the serial murderer who is stalking the women of Kiev. Rasia, being a top journalist for the Kiev Post, decides to pursue the killer on her own, and reap the benefits of his sacrifice. For one thing, she is disgusted with what he is doing to women, and she believes he needs to die. But on the other hand, she'll get off killing the murderer anyway, so it's a no-brainer for her to chase him down. Her entire way of thinking is skewed, and any good she does is just the inevitable part of a sick ripple effect.

Now, back to the 'witch' aspect of things. Rasia is not just a witch by practice alone, she is a witch by blood. The line goes back for generations, and let me tell you, these are some husband-killing, child-sacrificing witches. She has been taught by the writings of her Grandmother Anfisa in the sacred Book that if a witch were to sustain a vampire bite, she would not only live eternally, but she would have power unsurpassed, as well. This is the driving force behind everything Rasia Engres does in her life, from her career choice to every last sacrifice; if there is a true vampire walking the earth, Rasia intends to find him.

Once she finds him, however, he must bite her, and she is pretty sure that it isn't easy to dictate who a vampire will bite. The good news is she is stunningly beautiful, she is accomplished, and as a witch, she is somewhat resistant to DeSai's more hypnotic qualities. Rasia is a confident woman with a strong mindset: Come hell or high water, she will get her bite.

She doesn't sound like someone who would have enough nurturing ability in her little finger to birth and raise a child, but by the end of the book, it is obvious that is exactly what she is going to do. It is here that I realized it was important to soften her up a bit, no matter how little. Yes, she is going to have a baby, but she is still a terrible person; I felt the best approach was for her to begin to rue the killing of Cyril, and maybe she realizes that she loved him just a bit. This is a burden that Rasia Engres must bear for her own eternity.

'In the Depths' and 'Witches Immortal' are basically the story of a vampire and a witch who make a baby; the trilogy will culminate with his birth and life in book three. Cyril DeSai was a manipulative vampire who actually began to take over the world. Rasia Engres is the beautiful witch who rips it all from his hands. Their child will put them both to shame. When discussing only Rasia, however, she can stand on her own two feet in any situation, with no exception. While I despised her as a person, I loved her as a character, and she was actually one of my favorites to write about. She will continue on in book three, and fans will get to see how life, and its random series of events, brings everyone to their knees, including vampires and witches.

I had fun writing 'Witches Immortal', and I hope you get just as much enjoyment out of it when you read it. I found it entertaining to develop the character of Rasia, taking over with her from 'In the Depths', and I don't believe you will be disappointed. The woman certainly is evil through and through.

LUCIEN'S REIGN

(DeSai Trilogy Book 3)
ISBN-10: 069272219X ISBN-13: 978-0692722190

Supernatural Thriller

The third and final book in my DeSai Trilogy is entitled 'Lucien's Reign', and it tells the story of the culmination of Cyril DeSai and Rasia Engres in their son, Lucien. Ultimately, Lucien's existence has been the key all along; his mother Rasia and even his father Cyril were only mere pawns in the game the Powers are playing. This final installment chronicles his life until he finally comes into complete power at the age of eighteen.

At the very beginning of the book, Rasia is in the throes of labor. Now, to readers who are familiar with her character from reading the first two, she is a hard, dark woman with nothing but evil intent in her heart. She has murdered the vampire Cyril DeSai, but not until after they have made passionate love. Pregnant with his child, she picked up his mantle and continued on as his wife and head of the new DeSai family, which he has been creating.

Rasia is aware that her son is something of a 'chosen' one. He has a purpose set firmly in stone by the Powers, and the fact that he is the most horrific of breeds, a cross between a vampire and a witch, makes him dangerous from the beginning. At times, you may notice that she is apprehensive when it comes to him, almost as if she is afraid of him. Because she is so hateful, it is a bit satisfying, in a sense, for her to be fearful of another, particularly her own child.

Her trepidation turns out to be justified: Lucien is the son of Satan himself; not a man, but an animal with insatiable appetites that he cannot even begin to comprehend. So basic are these instincts, and so powerful, that Lucien doesn't even give them a second's consideration. He simply does what feels good and what pleases him at the moment.

The birth of Lucien Cerebus DeSai is nothing but a threat to Rasia, and this interferes with her affection. She is afraid of the Powers, as she should be, so she confirms. Otherwise, as far as her son goes, he is nothing more than the one who would take the rule from her hands; she would eventually be his slave. She hates him, deep inside; there is really not an ounce of true affection in her soul for the boy she carries and births.

I wanted a certain level of normalcy and balance to remain in the world in this book, even though the majority of the population are vampires. The only way to accomplish this was through the mean-spirited Rasia; I had to play up her mothering instincts, and I had to make Cyril's family dream become her dream as well. Only in this way would she raise Lucien with the iron fist necessary for him to become an effective family head. All character defects aside, she does the best she can; she schools him herself and basically keeps him isolated, with the exception of a single female friend, who eventually becomes his betrothed.

Isabella Scarlet Gilliam is the daughter of Patrick, the first bitten by DeSai while on a scuba diving trip when DeSai began to build his family. She is the voice of reason and the rock of stability throughout Lucien's life; she knows him like no other, bearing witness to, and keeping all of his secrets. She adores him as the night adores the moon, and she looks forward to the day she will be his wife. She, like Lucien, is a 'half-breed'. Her mother is human a majority of Isabella's life. Lucien is unaware of his witch vampire lineage until later in the book, as you will see.

Isabella also suffers an abundance of heartache and grief when it comes to her love. At one point, Lucien goes through a sort of 'vampire puberty' that sends him off on insane sexual tangents. For a long period, he completely puts Isabella out of his life, and she attempts to go on with her own, her love continuing to burn. But her own mother Rose will not allow her to have a relationship with another because Isabella's marriage to Lucien is inevitable; it is the will of the Powers. The girl must bear her burdens alone.

I should also mention the other signs of wickedness that Lucien displays in his life, though more often than not, are only visible to you, the reader. Rasia knows he is sick, but she is unaware of all he really does; he is deceitful and conniving like no other child before him, and he hides his fun and games well. Rasia finds herself on her knees before the powers, even asking to end her own son's life, to no avail. The Powers demand that she fulfill her given task: To raise the boy to maturity and power.

Writing 'Lucien's Reign' was a good time; I was able to really cut loose in a lot of areas regarding the true enormity of Lucien's evil character while attempting to help readers embrace any iota of humanity that he may possess. I believe I also dealt justice wisely to Rasia for all of her sins, and I think that the reader will agree. For those who have read this book, or the entire series, I do hope you had as much fun with these sick characters as I have.

ABOUT THE AUTHOR

I am a father of two beautiful children, Jon and Kim. They are my motivating forces; they are the lighthouse in this vast ocean. In this life, they are the air that I breathe; they are the oasis in this desert of uncertainty. They are my greatest joy in life, and my number one priority. I have a long list of hobbies, and I attribute that to my lust for life! I like to surround myself with positive people, who share the same interests. Family values, the arts, outdoors, nature, and travel are tops on my list. I embrace attending cultural and artistic events because I believe dramatic self-expression is the window to the soul. I wear my heart on my sleeve, and I still believe in chivalry, and I always treat people the way I want to be treated.

www.rwkclark.com

AUG 1 6 2018

PP Rot 9/19

GT 1/20

TR MN 7/20

CPSIA information can be obtained
at www.ICGtesting.com
Printed in the USA
FSHW02n0739220718
50783FS

9 781948 312011